LIFE'S
VIGNETTES

Also by Roger and Dianne Miller,
Meeting Christ in Scripture, Paulist Press, 1979

LIFE'S
VIGNETTES

A Collection of Short Stories
Covering One Man's Life

Roger Miller

iUniverse, Inc.
New York Bloomington

Life's Vignettes

A Collection of Short Stories Covering One Man's Life

iUniverse books may be ordered through booksellers or by contacting:

iUniverse
1663 Liberty Drive
Bloomington, IN 47403
www.iuniverse.com
1-800-Authors (1-800-288-4677)

ISBN: 978-1-4401-8292-1 (pbk)
ISBN: 978-1-4401-8293-8 (ebk)

Printed in the United States of America

iUniverse rev. date:10/29/09

PREFACE

As my family of two sons and four daughters were growing up, I recognized I should be documenting many of the cute little vignettes of daily humor occurring around me, but time and the demands of parenthood just didn't support this task. With the advent of the Word Processor, and retirement time became less of a constraint.

So one day early in the 1980s, I began collecting vignettes.

This is not meant to be a complete chronological autobiography. This is a partial collection of various short stories. Short stories about humorous family incidents, significant milestones in my life, humble attempts at poetry and some family statistics. Some of the poetry is original, some of the poetry are children jingles that were learned at 10 years of age, authors unknown.

ACKNOWLEDGMENTS

My thanks to my wife Dianne, of 55 years, for her encouragement, and to long time friend Mark Royston, author of several enjoyable books, for his help and support.

COVER GRAPHICS
by
Sarah Apke

Table of Contents

TABLE OF CONTENTS BY CHAPTER CONTENTS

CHAPTER 1
My Childhood
(the 1930's)

A GRANDFATHER I NEVER KNEW

I never met the man. He died six years before I was born. My mother said he was a very opinionated person. Family pictures show a tall self-assured looking individual. On Sunday mornings he would walk alone the one mile to Mass at the Holy Cross church at North Prairie, Minnesota, smoking a cigar. My mother said she would always walk right behind him so she could smell the cigar smoke, which she thought smelled good. When he didn't want his children to understand what he was saying, he spoke German to my Grandmother. During World War I, he got into violent arguments with a male schoolteacher who boarded in their farmhouse.

Apparently my maternal grandfather was pro-German, and this position infuriated the schoolteacher. During the building of the dam over the Mississippi at Little Falls, Minnesota, he hired himself and his team out to move earth. One day while trimming a horse's hoof, he cut his finger badly. When his co-workers recommended he see a doctor, he "brushed" off the suggestion, stating the cut was nothing. He was apparently a he-man type that didn't feel he needed to pamper himself.

A couple of weeks later they amputated his arm and within a short time my grandfather was dead of blood poisoning.

I think I've always been a little unhappy with him for dying before I was born and before I had a chance to meet and know him.

These vignettes are just a brief sharing of this grandfather's life and thoughts with his family, grandchildren and great grandchildren.

MY EARLIEST MEMORY

(Circa 1932)

It was 1932, and I remember squeezing through the stockade fence. The convicts in the stone blockhouse were yelling at me through their barred windows. Finally a guard came out of the blockhouse and asked me how I had gotten into the yard. He took me to the sally port at the stockade entrance and manipulated the gates in a manner that was meant to show me that when the outside gate to the sally port was closed, the inside gate would open, but both gates would not open at the same time to let me out. This little demonstration was meant to impress upon me that if I ever squeezed through the fence into the stockade again, I would never ever get out. Totally impressed and scared to death, I ran home on my 2 1/2 half year old legs, never to return to that awful place again. Six months later we moved to the mainland. I never again had the opportunity or temptation to try to squeeze into the Santa Catalina Island Avalon jail stockade.

A FIVE YEAR OLD'S APPENDECTOMY

I remember being taken to the doctor because of stomach pains, then on to St. Mary's hospital in Long Beach at 10th and Linden. I was put in a room lit by a weak over the headboard lamp. I was operated on in the next few hours and while Doctor Benledge was removing my appendix it burst and I got peritonitis, which caused my stomach to swell up as if I was nine months pregnant. My bowels stopped working and froze up and I became a very sick five year old with an extremely high fever. I lingered for days with my infected and enlarged stomach. Of course I remember very little, this part of my story comes from my mother who retold it time and again. Without the miracle drugs of today, the only course of action for that much infection and high fever in 1935 was numerous hot packs on my stomach and enemas to try and get my bowels to move. My mother related the nurses kept putting hot packs on my stomach which were so hot they carried them into my room balanced on wooden sticks to keep from burning their hands. They had my stomach well lubricated so my skin was not burnt. Doctor Bendledge said he had done all he could think to do. My mother prayed and related that the doctor said, "Where there is a will, there is a way." Then one afternoon, a Nun came running out of the room saying my bowels had burst – and I guess that meant there was stool all over everything. After my bowels started to work, my fever came down and the swelling subsided. I was in the hospital for over thirty days, and only after I was getting better do I remember anything. One day a Nun told me to tell my nurse she was a bad egg for something the nurse had failed to do - that I now no longer remember. I got the message mixed up and told the nurse she was a rotten egg. The nurse feigned hurt and hurried out of the room, and I felt real bad about calling her a bad name. I loved it when my Mom came to visit and read me the comics. As a result of that operation and the massive scar it left I always had weak stomach muscles which didn't give me a nice flat stomach. My brother kidded me that I had a potbelly.

SUNDAY DRIVES

Sunday drives through the orange groves of Southern California were a family ritual. We had a late 1920's sedan that had an emergency brake handle behind the front seat straddling the drive shaft. My father had removed the brake handle and mechanism to repair it. The resulting hole in the rear floorboard was about two by six inches. My brother and I entertained our selves during many long rides by dropping wadded paper out the hole and then jumping to the rear window to see where the bouncing wad of paper finally came to rest. This little diversion for two active young boys made many a Sunday drive far more interesting and less boring

SISTER SAID

Sister, at Holy Innocents Church in Long Beach, told all of us seven year olds that when we receive our first Holy Communion, we were to bow our heads and say the Our Father. Then we were to rise and return to our seats. I did it just like Sister said.

Being told nothing to the contrary, I continued to say the Our Father each time I received communion thereafter.

As the years passed, I began to notice that those around me always seemed to say their Our Fathers extremely fast. I was always the last to get up from the communion rail. It really began to bug me! I was saying my Our Father as fast as I could, yet all around me seemed to say theirs faster. Even my mother!

One day I asked the question, and received the answer, "What Our Father are you talking about?" It was somewhat akin to learning about Santa Claus. Nothing can be so injurious to a conscientious person's faith in the church's teaching authority than to learn you have not been given all the salient facts.

For example, when attending a young married couples retreat during lent one year, the retreatants were served, by the nuns, coffee, tea, donuts and rolls at all the morning and evening breaks. This really bugged me. For as good adult Catholics, we were expected to fast during Lent--and not eat between meals. Why were we subjected to all this food and temptation when we couldn't partake. Only pregnant women and those over 55 were exempt-there were only a couple in attendance. Indignant, I asked the question at an evening question and answer period. The retreat master smiled and informed us that a loophole exists in Cannon Law that allows one to eat some food when partaking of drink. The reasoning being that centuries ago, drink was commonly wine or other spirits, and it was recognized that it was good to take a little food with strong drink.

Again, I had failed to receive the whole story from the many who had taught me my faith.

KRESSES 5 AND 10 CENT STORE

It was 1937, my younger brother and I would accompany my mother on the bus to downtown Long Beach, California, for one of her bi-monthly shopping trips. Lunchtime was always special. The Kress building had a basement lunch counter that sold a bowl of soup for a nickel with all the oyster crackers you could eat. I would fill up my soap bowl with those wonderful round little crackers and savor the soap of the day. To this day, I love oyster crackers in my soup. I often ask for more so I can fill my bowl with those wonderful round delights enjoyed so long ago. It has been pointed out that dumping crackers in one's soap is not the height of etiquette, but I don't care, a part of me simply loves oyster crackers in my soup.

MOM'S PURCHASE

When my maternal grandfather died in the early twenties, the Minnesota Burggraff family farm went to his widow, Grandma Susan. It was to be run by the oldest son, my Uncle Justus (Uncle Butch). There was no cash to make an equitable adjustment to the surviving five daughters, so Uncle Justus promised to pay off his sisters as he was able. In the late thirties, Uncle Justus sent my mother two hundred dollars.

In those days a couple could get a Federal Housing Authority loan if they owned the land. My father had been reluctant to go into debt buying a piece of land. So unbeknownst to my dad, my mother took her two hundred dollars, chose a lot and bought it. With the fact accomplished, mom then talked dad into getting a $5,200 loan and building the house at 3569 Gaviota Avenue, Long Beach, California.

A couple years later my dad died abruptly of a blood clot on the brain. He had a ten thousand dollar life insurance policy. Mom paid off the remaining house loan and that decision served her very well by keeping a roof over her head until her death in 1991.

DADDY COME! MOMMIE?

My father died abruptly of a blood clot on the brain on my Mother's birthday on October 21, 1940. I was ten years old, brother David was eight, and brother LeRoy was two.

Each evening LeRoy would climb up on my Dad's lap when he came home from work. If my dad was eating late, little LeRoy would sit on his lap during his whole meal.

LeRoy couldn't understand the sudden absence of his father. My mother told him that his daddy had gone far far away on a train. This seemed a good idea at the time to help this child understand why his father was no longer coming home at night.

For almost a year afterward, each time LeRoy heard a train whistle, he'd say, "Daddy come Mommie? Daddy come?"

AUNT JUSTINA'S ROOTBEER

Aunt Justina was my mothers oldest sister. In the 1930's, she and Uncle Tom Trutwin lived on a small rented farm south of North Prairie, Minnesota. My mother tried to go back to visit her home once every two or three years. Some of my earliest memories are of these visits to Minnesota. We would stay at Aunt Justina's for three or four days, then visit Aunt Tally in Bowlus, then Uncle Butch (Justus Burggraff) on his farm outside of Bowlus, and finally Aunt Delia in Royalton.

Each place has a special memory. On a hot sultry summer afternoon nothing was more wonderful than to have Aunt Justina draw a cool bucket of homemade bottled root beer out of the cooling water of her well and offer us a glass. I could have drunk a gallon of that delicious beverage, but it had to be shared with my family and many cousins. I always wished for more.

1930-Roger Miller at 6 months

1930-Ursula and Roy holding son Roger

1930-Roy Miller beside his 1928 Star Roadster

1933-Roger in his 1933 Run-a-Bout

1933-Roger with German Sheppard Ginger

1934-Roger and brother David with Grandpa
Joe and Grandma Mary Miller

1939-Roger 9, David 7, and LeRoy 2

CHAPTER 2
My Adolescence
(The 1940's)

BIG BUG

One day in 1940, my three year old brother excitedly ran into the house with the exclamation, "Mommie, come see big bug, big bug Mommie!" My mother hurried into the back yard to check on what this little child was so excitedly describing. Crawling across the driveway was a grown desert tortoise. We soon found out that Slow Joe, as we named him, had a wandering streak. Fearful that he would get run over by a car we children were continually cautioned to always close the yard gate. Neighbors soon learned who to call when he did get out. For years, Slow Joe wandered our back yard, ate lettuce, other greens and dandelions. He hibernated in a corner of our garage from November until March of each year. Not knowing if Slow Joe could swim, one day my brother David and I filled my mother's washtub with water and placed the tortoise in it. He immediately sank to the bottom. We quickly concluded he couldn't swim but we weren't sure how long a desert tortoise could hold his breath, so after a few minutes we took him out and he crawled away apparently unharmed.

When my mother died in 1991, the first question asked by relatives and friends was who would take care of old Slow Joe. I inherited the task. Each fall I make sure he has a dry place to hibernate and in the warm months I make sure he has plenty of his favorite treat, lettuce. Slow Joe in return keeps my backyard free of dandelions. When I'm working in the backyard he often crawls between my legs and then stops and waits for an offering of his favorite treat. Today when one or more of our twentyeight grandchildren visit, he's now become their favorite big bug. At a family reunion in August 1994, in North Prairie, Minnesota, numerous cousins came up to me and said, "I've been meaning to ask, whatever happen to old Slow Joe the turtle?" When old Slow Joe wandered into our yard in 1940, the edges of his shell showed signs that someone had drilled holes in the edge of is shell and tried to tether him in his distant past. Our family has never tried to tether him. He looks the same and about as old today as he did that day he came to us fifty-five years ago. Old Slow Joe may well out last us all.

PAINTING A RED SAIL BOAT

My twelve year old first cousin, Glenn, was painting a red sail boat. I was a couple years younger and I decided to take a small stick and help him. He objected and told me to stop. I continued to dip the small stick into the red paint and to smear a little on the boat. He pushed me away and I flicked a little paint at him. At this point he picked up the can of red paint and dumped it on my head. I then ran for home, which was about one and a half blocks away. I took a short cut down an alley where two city employees were collecting trash. When they saw me running, crying and dripping what appeared to be blood they became very concerned and called for me to stop. They then started to chase me and I cut between some houses to the next street and continued to run toward home. Needless to say when my mother saw me she let out a cry of shock and concern until she realized it was paint and not blood. My punishment was immediate for I had to stand for almost an hour while my mother used solvents to try and get the paint out of my hair. My mother and my aunt concluded that while my cousin had over reacted, I really had brought this incident upon myself. As it is with boys of that age, in less than a week all was forgotten and I was back playing with my cousin Glenn.

THE BRAYTON THEATER

It was the late1930's and a quarter was a lot of money. It cost a nickel to ride the bus to the Brayton Theater in Long Beach, California. Nine cents to get in, a nickel to go home and six cents were left for candy. When the cost of admission was raised to ten cents we all took that in stride. But when the admission went to eleven cents, that was just too much, for we no longer had enough left for a nickel candy bar. We had to be satisfied with four penny candies.

We all felt the Brayton Theater had a very strange manager. All of us that entered at noon on Saturday were given a candy bar as we left after the double feature of cowboy westerns and serials. The problem was that the manager always ran out of candy bars before the last kid was out of the theater. So just as soon as the movie was over, there was a mad stampede to get to the door to make sure we got our candy bar before he ran out. We never did figure out the method to his madness until we were young adults and wished that the noisy kids would leave the theater so we could enjoy the movie.

While standing at the bus stop my brother David, my cousin Glenn and I would decide who would be the good guys and the bad guys when we got home and we could strap on our guns and cowboy costumes.

SLEEPING IN MOM'S ROOM

After my Dad died in October, 1940, David and I were both so shook up that we wanted to sleep in Mom's room. It lasted for quite a while, until she weaned us out of the idea. The scars on the personality are something that last for a long time.

GRANDMA'S MENDING

As a ten year old I remember my Grandmother calling out, "Rogers, come thread my needle."

Will Rogers was famous at the time and I guess his name came more readily to her mind than a simple, Roger. My youthful sharp eyes always made for a faster threading of her needles. Grandma did all the family mending, especially the socks. She would slip a sock over a wooden ball or a light bulb and produce a wonderfully soft and neatly mended patch.

As a young husband, when I informed my wife that a favorite sock needed to be mended, I was summarily told to throw them out. The demands of young children didn't allow her time to mend socks.

However, in subsequent years when a favorite sock needed mending, I still take a light bulb, thread a needle and mend the hole. In no way can I make a soft patch like Grandma Burggraff, but I have been able to prolong the life of many a favorite pair of socks, much to the continuing amusement of my wife and children.

SUMMER ON THE FARM

I was ten years old in the spring of 1941. My recently widowed mother, myself and two younger brothers, David and LeRoy, moved to Minnesota that spring. We were assisted in our drive from California by my mother's older brother, Uncle Butch (Justus Burggraff). We stayed in a house located across the road from this uncle's farm. The property had been purchased by my uncle for the farming acreage. A house, barn and sheds were on the property. The house's second floor was partially unfinished. The kitchen on the first floor had been used as a winter chicken coop and was a mess-which my mother and Grandma Burggraff had to immediately clean up. The barn was used to store alfalfa and the sheds were used to store his thrashing machine and a wonderful old diesel tractor that provided a 36" flywheel take-off for the long belt powering the thrashing rig. It was said by my cousins that this old tractor could climb a tree if it could get the proper traction.

My Uncle Butch's (Justus Burggraff) family was my first exposure to a working farm family. Their family consisted of the following children with their approximate ages:

Bernadette	20	
Margaret	19	(Bocky)
Charles1	8	(Charlie)
Method	17	(Tuddy)
Justus	13	
Adrain	11	(Ati)
William	7 (	Billy)
Joseph	5	(Jo Jo)

The two girls helped Aunt Barbara and Grandma Susan in the kitchen, whereas the boys were assigned outside chores by my uncle or one of the older boys. Failure to comply with the chore assignments was backed up by the older boy's threat to tell my uncle and his ultimate application of his razor strap. I can't recall my uncle giving David or I any chore assignments or scoldings.

My uncle was an inventor of sorts. He could often be found in his machine shop tinkering with one of his inventions that raised the plow shear up when encountering a large rock when plowing, thus preventing damage to the plow shear blade. He tried to sell his invention, but he couldn't find any buyers.

I finished out my fifth grade year in a one room school house located next to the Holy Cross Church in North Prairie, Minnesota, about a mile from the farm. Even though the remaining school year was less than three months, this old time educational experience left a lasting impression on me. A row for each of the first and second grades, half a row each for the third and fourth grades, a row for the fifth grade, half a row each for the sixth and seventh grades and a row for the eighth occupied the entire first floor of the two story school house. Playing "any any over" over the wood shed during recess was a new experience as was a school room where eight grades were being taught by one teacher in one room. Also a new experience was the multi-holed out house used by all the kids.

The summer vacation starts early in farming country for the children are all needed on the farms to help with cutting new hay, plowing and the harvest. So by the first of June, school was out for the summer.

When I was eleven I learned a lesson about harming other creatures that I have never forgotten. That summer my mother finally agreed to buy my younger brother and me a Daisy BB rifle thinking that it would be safe enough around a farm's open fields. My brother and I shot at many inanimate targets in the ensuing days. One afternoon I was by myself looking for targets of opportunity when I spotted a sparrow sitting on the top ridge of the barn. A long and difficult shot for a Daisy BB rifle. I took very careful aim and squeezed the trigger. At first I had elation at hitting the target and then shock as I watched the bird flutter to the ground. I walked up to the injured bird fluttering on the ground and felt terrible. That little creature had done nothing to me and yet I had shot and injured it. I remember walking away feeling awful, never again to shoot at another living creature with that BB gun. I went back later and apparently the bird had recovered and flown away.

Living across from a working farm was a very new experience for a city boy who at ten hadn't done much more than to pick up his room and once a week sweep out the garage and mow a front and back lawn. David and I would go across the road to visit my cousin Adrian who was also ten (we both turned eleven that summer), and find him performing an assignment of chores like cleaning cow manure out of the barn, or feeding the chickens, or actually sitting on a Farmal tractor plowing a field. To be required to work a whole day without time to PLAY was just about inconceivable to me. My younger brother David and I would tag along with Adrian as he did his chores and distract him or just get in the way much to the exasperation of my uncle who would have preferred that we just left his chore performing son alone. On occasions we did have time in the late afternoons for a game of hide and seek. It was great fun to run through my aunt's garden grab a handful of carrots and hide in the corn field among the large cornstalks, waiting for who ever was *it* to find us.

Once when brother David and I were alone and bored, we repeatedly slid down one of the straw stacks, much to the distress of my Uncle Butch. We city boys didn't know that straw stacks were carefully topped with a specially constructed straw crown to cause the rain water to run off the straw pile and not soak in, thus causing the straw to rot. My uncle sternly explained how we must not play on his straw crowns. The time it took him to repair the crown was reprimand enough.

So we moved into the old barn where a whole loft of alfalfa was stored. We found the alfalfa held together real well so we dug a room under the alfalfa and called it our fort. Never considering the room might collapse. But the room was dark, so we found a candle and lit it for light. It never occurred to us that the alfalfa might ignite, thus burning down the old barn and a loft full of alfalfa.

My uncle was always apprehensive that I and David might get hurt around an operating farm.

Each morning my chore was to walk a quarter of a mile along a lane and across the dirt road to my uncle's barn where I filled a two quart can with fresh warm milk. I would dress at the break of day and walk barefooted to this early rendezvous. Occasionally I tried to get up very early to beat my cousins to the barn, but one or more of them were always there ahead of me milking the cows. One of the older cousins was in charge of the milking. Sometimes if I got too close to cousins my own age I would get squirted with warm milk. Utter squirting can be fun for ten year olds, but all too often the milk soured on the floor and on our clothing making a smelly sticky mess. Usually the older boys would stop the milk squirting before too much milk was wasted and too much of a mess was made. After a short visit I would return with my can of milk and our family would have breakfast. On humid hot summer days, I felt this was the best part of the day. Even the mosquitoes were still asleep.

The house we stayed in was used by a bootlegger during prohibition to make liquor. The place was raided when the basement was full of barrels of liquor. The Revenue Officers broke open all the barrels with axes and let the liquor pour out onto the basement floor. My cousins pointed out with pride the stain on the basement wall that was made by all of the spilled illegal liquor.

This house had no electricity nor a working water well. Even the outhouse was falling apart and much to our unhappiness frequented by many flies, wasps and bees. Every couple of days we had to haul water in a large milk can. Our 1936 Chevrolet had a running board on which we could balance the water can. We would fill the can up at my Uncle's pump and lift it onto the running board. Then my brother and I would lean out the window and steady it while my mother slowly drove the quarter mile back to our house. We used kerosene lamps for light at night. Often the kerosene would run out near the end of the month and we would all have to go to bed when it grew dark. We then had to wait until my mother's Social Security check came before additional kerosene could be bought. Once family friends from California visited us near the end of the month and my mother was quite embarrassed when it grew dark and we had no more kerosene for the lamps.

Somehow it never occurred to me that we were poor. We just ran out of money to buy kerosene for a few days the last of each month. There was always enough food to eat. When you live on a farm or by a farm, there was always plenty of milk and vegetables.

My mother insisted we all take baths every Saturday afternoon whether we felt we needed them or not. My mother would fill a bathtub in my uncle's pump house with warm water. The pump house was about twenty-five yards from his farmhouse. The bathtub was filled with water via a bucket from the pump head and warm water also by bucket from the kitchen stove. Then she would take her bath and bathe my two year old brother. Next my brother David who was two years younger than I would be bathed in the same water, then I would take my bath in the dirty cold soapy water that remained.

My uncle's farm did have electricity, but no plumbing. Water was available, as I mentioned, from a cool one hundred foot deep well that was brought to the surface via an electric pump. . My uncle's toilet facilities was an "outhouse" with two lower level holes for the younger children and a couple of holes for the adults. Sometimes I would go into the outhouse and my uncle, aunt or grandmother would all be sitting on a hole. I would use whatever vacant one that was available. I also opted to use my Uncle's outhouse rather than our bee and wasp infested one across the road.

The main interstate roads eight miles away were paved, but all of the county roads were dirt. Consequently our car often got very dusty. With no water at our house we could not conveniently wash the car. But we could drive down the road to another farm where their entrance lane forded a creek. We would then stand in the cool calf deep creek and wash the car. We didn't bother to ask permission for we knew the farmer would not mind us using a little of his creek water.

Cousin Adrian who was my age explained to me the "H" stick shifting pattern of our 1936 Chevrolet car. After much practicing and then much begging, my mother finally allowed me to back the car out of the garage. Then after more begging she allowed me to drive the car down the quarter mile lane to the county road. There was a very large tree right in the middle of the lane mid-way between the house and the road. That tree was my first great driving challenge. I never did hit it, but it sure gave me much strife.

Six miles from my Uncle's farm was Bowlus, Minnesota. The local merchants sponsored a movie in the town park each Saturday evening in the summer. We all looked forward to this weekly gathering which had one large drawback! These were the days before Mosquito abatement. The evenings were most always hot and humid. I would arrive at the park with a piece of heavy canvas the size of a blanket. I would wrap myself in the blanket leaving only a small hole to peek through to watch the movie. Sad to say this protection still did not completely stop the Mosquitoes which bit right through the canvas. How I ever sat and watched a whole movie that way on a hot and humid night I will never know.

During the day the Mosquitoes weren't too bad in and around the farmhouse and barn. But in the cooler dampness of the woods behind my uncle's farm they would surround us in frenzied biting clouds. Adrian and I would walk in the woods until the Mosquito cloud would get so thick that we could hardly breath, then we would run fifty yards, roll in the grass and then run another fifty yards until we had broken up and lost the cloud of Mosquitoes. We would continue walking through the woods until the cloud again formed and got so thick we couldn't stand them--then we would again run, roll and run. We continued this procedure until we were through the woods.

In the evening, we showed such a small amount of light via the lamps that we did not draw too many Mosquitoes into the house.

If we wanted to go fishing we merely walked out the back door of the house through a woods, along a bottom land pasture and there after a half a mile was the mighty Mississippi river. We didn't go swimming in the river or any of its backwater sloughs for this was an area of snapping turtles who had very impressive beaks. An "old wife's tale" related that if a snapping turtle got hold of your toe it wouldn't let go until the sun set that day. A tale which I believed at the age of ten. The area also had bloodsucking leaches which I felt were more distasteful than the turtles. Also in the woods back of the house were choke cherries in the late summer. I never totally developed a taste for these small red canning delights.

The farm just north of my uncle's was owned by the Herman Wiener family. Herman had a large bull of questionable temperament that could high jump over all the barbed wire fences on the Wiener farm. Occasionally we found the Wiener bull wandering around in our barnyard when we got up in the morning. My mother and us kids were very afraid of the bull and stayed in the house until he wandered off or until one of the Wiener family came and led it with a nose ring restraint pole back to their farm. One morning my grandmother got tired of the bull grazing in our barnyard and keeping us all "penned up" in the house and she went after it with a broom. She was able to chase it off while my mother yelled at her to come back in the house before she was gored by the bull. Occasionally when we were walking down to the Mississippi River or in the woods at the back of our house we would come across this bull that had a real wanderlust.

My mother had rented out her house in Long Beach for a year. She had planned to stay in Minnesota through the winter of 1941 and 1942. Then in the spring of 1942 she was going to decide if she was going to stay in Minnesota or go back to California. But my older cousin, Jimmy Booth, had just graduated from High School and signed up for an aircraft mechanic training class in Downey for the fall of 1941. He needed a ride to California. Also Jimmy provided older male company for our family on our drive back to California. My mother felt a little pushed by her sister Tally to take Jimmy to California. I have often wondered if I would still have such positive memories about life on the farm if we had spent a cold Minnesota winter in that farmhouse. It definitely would have been an experience. I really don't know how my mother would have kept that house warm during the cold winter. It had a fireplace and a wood burning stove, but no good central heating system.

None the less that spring and summer of 1941 left a eleven year old, who had just lost his father the previous October, with wonderful memories and experiences that have never been forgotten.

I'M AFRAID I'LL JUMP

I was ten years old, and younger brother David was eight. We were standing on the Bowlus, Minnesota, depot platform waiting for the daily Soo Line mail train from Minneapolis. As the old laboring steam engine rounded the final curve coming into the station, David ran over and stood behind some barrels. I asked him why he was doing that and he said, "I'm afraid I'll jump in front of the engine."

I looked at him and wondered what kind of a crazy fear was that?

I had always felt I was the anxious one and David was the happy-go-lucky one of the family. But as the years progressed, I learned that David was much more insecure than I. My mother told me, David was absolutely lost when I was drafted into the army.

UNCLE HEINIE'S SNOWMOBILE

His name was Henry Booth. He was the husband of my mother's sister Tally (Natalia). Uncle Heinie was the one man Post Master in Bowlus, Minnesota. The post office was one small building across the town square from the train depot.

David and I loved to walk to the depot from Aunt Tally's house, a couple blocks, and wait for the Soo Line's noon steam locomotive to arrive with the daily mail. When Uncle Heinie retrieved the mailbag from the mail car, he would walk it over to his small post office and begin to sort all the post office box mail. Then he would climb into his Model A Ford and begin delivery to the routes to the outlying farms.

I was always fascinated by the simplistic rural address of my Uncle Butch's farm. It was just, J. Burggraff, Bowlus, Minn., Route 1. Uncle Heinie knew everyone on Route 1, so no more detail was necessary.

Uncle Heinie had a marvelous old half track Model T Ford, with tractor threads on the rear and skis on the front, with a small iron pot bellied stove in the front right next to the driver's seat. I would have loved to see it run, but taking out a snowmobile without any snow on the ground was out of the question. So I would visit the town garage where it was stored in the summer and dream of what a wonderful adventure it would be to ride in such an outstanding machine, going down the cold iced and snow bound country roads.

AUNT DELLA'S OLD HOTEL

On subsequent trips to Minnesota in the middle 1940's we would stay a few days with my mother's various sisters and brother. We would arrive and stay with Aunt Della in Royalton for a few days, then go on to Bowlus and stay with Aunt Tally, then Uncle Butch on his farm a mile north of North Prairie, and finally with Aunt Justina whose farm was a couple miles south of North Prairie.

Aunt Della rented and lived in a small old hotel for a few years on the northern edge of Royalton, just south of a graveyard. She always had plenty of room, for she would just open a closed upstairs room, throw a mattress on the floor and we had a place to sleep that night. Downstairs Aunt Della and Uncle Jim had their bedroom. Their kids occupied various other upstairs rooms. Also downstairs was a large front room, dinning room, and a sizable kitchen. A hand pump in the middle of the backyard supplied their water. An outhouse at the back of the property finished out the utility requirements.

A small river flows through Royalton, with a great swimming hole at the south end of town. Visits to the other relatives didn't provide such nice swimming accommodations.

Highlights of our Aunt Tally visits were meeting the daily Soo Lines freight and mail deliveries at the Bowlus depot. Meeting the train was always a bit of a question since it was seldom on time.

Visits to Uncle Butch's farm exposed us to early morning milking in the barn, leaping into piles of hay from the top of the hay barn and chasing the cows home from the pasture in the late afternoon.

My remaining impressions of Aunt Justina's farm was a newly built barn, and root beer cooling in her well.

TWO BLACK EYES

Sister Helenia said, "Roger Miller if you come into this classroom again with two black eyes, you are going to the office!"

The dreaded office where Sister Superior held life and death sway over those who were sent there. This admonishment to a eleven year old didn't give any clear direction for future conduct. No way did I want two black eyes again. My classmate slid into third base which I was covering, I said, "You're out!" and he said, "No I'm not," and Pow-Pow, he hit me in both eyes.

My father had died suddenly a year earlier, and the only direction I got from my mother was "don't fight." Sister Helenia didn't want me in her class, my mother didn't want me to fight or to defend myself and lurking in the main office building was the dreaded Sister Superior. What to do, what to do?

GRADE AND HIGH SCHOOLS I ATTENDED

I attended Kindergarten in 1935 at a temporary school at California Avenue and Wardlow Road in Long Beach while the Longfellow Grammar School was still being repaired from the 1933 Long Beach earthquake. And six months later I started first grade at the rebuilt Longfellow Grammar School at California Avenue and Bixby Road. I attended second, third, fourth and six months of the fifth grade at this same Longfellow Grammar School. My dad died in October 1940, and the family moved to Minnesota in the spring of 1941, where I finished my fifth grade year in a one-room schoolhouse in North Prairie. The one room had a row for each grade one through eight.

We returned to Long Beach in September 1941, where I was enrolled in the sixth grade at St. Anthony's Grammar school at Seventh Street and Linden in Long Beach, where I subsequently completed my eighth year of grammar school and four years of high school graduating in June 1948. I attended Long Beach City College for two years until June 1950, when I got a job for six months to try and earn some more money to continue my education. During this working period I was drafted in March 1951 and spent two years in the army, when I was released from active duty in April 1953.

"CAN I HAVE A SIP?" MOMMIE

Every summer my mother took us to Big Bear Lake for a week or two of tent camping. My Uncle Gene Brockway and Aunt Tracy (Therese) would also go at the same time. On one occasion, Mr. and Mrs. Ed Parr, who lived across the street from us, rented a cabin right on the lake. I always thought that it would be wonderful to be able to afford a cabin for a week rather then sleeping in a tent. One afternoon we went to visit the Parr family and mixed drinks were made for the adults. My youngest brother LeRoy, about three, asked his mother for a sip, which she gave him as she continued to take part in the adult discussions.

A short time later, one of the adults said, "Ursula, look at your son!" There little LeRoy was leaning against the wall with a glassy eyed stare holding an empty glass which he had managed to drain.

WW II RUBBER COLLECTIONS

World War II started for me on Sunday afternoon, December 7, 1941, when I came home from a movie and my mother told me we were probably going to be at war with Japan. She said they had bombed Pearl Harbor in the Hawaiian Islands. I didn't really know where the Hawaiian Islands were-out in the Pacific Ocean some place-I guessed. I knew there was a war over in Europe with the Germans, but we weren't fighting in it. The news didn't shake me up too much, for I didn't really appreciate what being at war meant at the age of eleven. First the president asked congress to declared war. Then the results of a war came closer to home as rationing became more involved. Things became in short supply, sugar was rationed, along with meats, butter, and other foodstuffs, and then came rubber tires, gasoline, cars, etc... The fighting was far away on Pacific islands whose names I couldn't pronounce. In downtown Long Beach was a newsreel theater that showed nothing but the news of where the fighting was going on. As an eleven year old I didn't like to pay to go into it because all they showed was news, no adventure story films, just news reels.

Then in the summer of 1942, rubber became in very short supply in the war effort. Gas stations were designated places to turn in used rubber and the donors would be reimbursed per pound. The heaviest rubber we could find were pieces of tires we found along the road. But soon everyone was picking up rubber and pieces along roads became less and less. Then one day as David, I and a friend were collecting along Cherry Avenue in Signal Hill, we stopped at a tire recapping plant and the owner said we could have pieces of rubber out back in fifty-three gallon drums. What a mint, what a treasure-we couldn't haul a fifty-three gallon drum, but we could fill up our wagons and haul them about a mile and a half to Don Slocum's gas station and get our loads weighed and paid for our labors. Of course, a treasure had to be spent, so as we trekked back to the recapping plant for another repeat trip we stopped at the Safeway and stocked up on candy and ice cream to sustained us. With pockets bulging with candy we walked the return mile and a half. Eventually the treasure ran out and we were forced to look farther and farther a field. One day we found a hard rubber tire and wheel from an abandoned oilrig. We tried to hack saw off the tire but we couldn't get it off and eventually gave up.

THE CRASH

Just after the start of World War II anti-aircraft guns were stationed all around the Long Beach, California airport. After our 1942 accomplishments in the Pacific made it readily apparent that the west coast was no longer in danger, the guns were removed and the gun emplacements abandoned. For twelve year olds, the underground barracks and the gun mounts were absolute magnets. We placed a two by four on the mount, and pretended the planes taking off were enemy aircraft and summarily tracked and shot at each one. Then we noticed a single engine fighter in a very steep dive and immediately swung our make believe gun around and tracked its progress toward the ground. We first shouted that we had hit it and it was going down. Then our yelling died down and we began to say, "You better pull up, pull up, he's not going to pull up! It's going to hit my house!" Another kid said, "No, it's going to hit my house!" For the next two seconds we all silently watched as the plane slammed into the ground, with a massive blast of fire and smoke. Each of us was afraid it may have hit our homes, so we hopped on our bikes and headed in that direction. As we rode the five blocks we became aware that the plane had hit beyond our homes. Of course we kept on riding our bikes toward the impact point. As I got a block beyond our house I noticed a parachute floating down. The pilot was picked up on Walnut Avenue, just south of Wardlow Road.

The plane had hit three blocks farther west on Brayton Avenue below Wardlow Road on the west side of the water department park storage tank. It missed a house with an elderly lady in it by a few feet. The pilot had a power failure in an F6F Hellcat, aimed the plane at a field south of the park and bailed out. He missed the field by almost a city block, but fortunately no one was hurt. The engine buried itself twelve feet down in the middle of Brayton Avenue. As I rode up, a kid who lived at Falcon and Wardlow was taking home a wing mounted .50 caliber machine gun, with an ammunition belt still dangling from the receiver. Military Police were just arriving and one saw him carrying the gun and had a tug-of-war pulling it away from him. The boy felt he found it and it was his. People were picking up souvenirs faster than the MPs could stop them. About this time my mother, knowing her boys would head for the excitement, arrived and immediately made us go home. By the time she escorted us back the area was all roped off and no one was allowed to pick up any more souvenirs. Of course as kids we did not appreciate the importance of the authorities' attempts to retrieve all of the plane's parts for subsequent accident investigations. For a twelve year old it was one of the more exciting days early in WW II.

KIDS POETRY

ONE FINE MORNING

One fine morning in the middle of the night,
Two dead boys came out to fight.
They met on the corner in the middle of the block,
In front of the apartment house on the vacant lot.
Back to back they faced each other,
Drew their swords and shot each other.
A deaf policeman heard the noise,
And came and shot the two dead boys.

LADIES AND GENTILES

Ladies and gentiles,
Reptiles and Crocodiles,
I come before you,
To stand behind you,
To tell you something I know nothing about.
Next Monday,
Which is Friday,
There will be a meeting for men,
Only for women to attend,
There will be no admission,
So pay at the door,
Bring your own seats,
And sit on the floor.
We'll meet at the round table,
You at this corner,
You at that corner,
And me at this corner.

CHAPTER 3
My Teen Years
(The 1940's)

A SOFT SPOT

During the 1940's I sold magazines, collected scrap rubber, delivered phone books, collected newspapers and delivered a daily newspaper. Initially the Los Angeles Herald Examiner part time and then the Long Beach Press Telegram on a daily route for about three years. However, I think that selling the Saturday Evening Post, the Collier, and the American magazines left the biggest impression on my psyche. The American Magazine cost a whole quarter, and its sale gave me the biggest profit. While I didn't sell too many at that high price, a couple sales really made my day. I can't begin to count the hours I spent going from door to door peddling these three magazines. So when our front door bell rings today, if my wife answers, she calls me for she knows I won't let a young peddler leave without buying something. When I look down at that expectant face, I somehow see myself fifty-five years ago looking up and hoping that this is the guy who will be willing to spend that quarter or today's inflated equivalent of that amount.

WILL J. REED BOY SCOUT PARK

In the 1940's, along the Los Angeles River near Long Beach, California, was a wonderful Boy Scout park. My widowed mother allowed my younger brother David and me to camp in this park because she felt we were properly supervised by our Scout Master and the park custodian. The park was about ten acres in size bordering the Los Angeles River on its west side. Initially it was not fenced, so that the northern boundary was somewhat vague to us boys. Often if we camped beyond the property line nothing was said.

The wilderness of trees and scrubs north of the park was ideal for "snipe-hunts". We were told a snipe was a wonderful little bird that flies low to the ground only at night. If one wishes to catch a snipe one must sit quietly with a net or blanket between two large trees or bushes and wait for the snipes to be chased into the net by your buddies. Of course some of us were more patient than others and would sit for an hour or more waiting for the snipe to show-up. Others were more impatient or afraid and would wander back to the campfire after fifteen or twenty minutes. When we did arrive back empty handed it was to much laughter and enjoyment from the other members of the troop. Every Tenderfoot scout went on at least an initial Snipe hunt.

Warm afternoons were spent hiking along the river bed and skinny-dipping in the sandy pools formed by the slowly flowing waters. This was still in the days before the Army Corps of Engineers paved the entire river to the ocean in concrete. In the spring, when the river ran high, even short raft trips were possible.

Often the adult leaders would spend the night in the custodian's house which was located on the east side of the property. They seldom wandered out into the park after dark unless we were being awfully noisy. The nights were ours to tell ghost stories and to crawl into our sleeping bags when we wanted too. For a twelve year old without a father these experiences left me with many wonderful memories.

When it was time for sleep, our senior patrol leader would call us all around the campfire. With our God given physiological capabilities we would all help put out the campfire flames. The only complaint coming from someone claiming that his shoe was being hit rather than the fire. Boys will be boys!

UPSIDE-DOWN IN WYOMING

It was sometime around June-July1945. My mother liked to visit her mother, brother and sisters in Minnesota about every two years. We had driven there during the latter part of the war years when gas rationing was still in effect. She had saved her wartime gas rationing coupons for about a year to get enough to make the trip. After about a month of visiting in Royalton, Bowlus and various family farms, it was time to head back to California. Grandma Burggraff was to accompany my mother, David, I and LeRoy.

My Uncle Butch (Justus Burggraff Sr.) cautioned my mother about her bald tires. All four tires had only minimal tread when we had left California. It was possible to accumulate gas coupons in the war years, but extremely difficult to get replacement tire coupons. Mom had her mindset on going to Minnesota, so she left on the trip with very poor tire treads on all four tires. Amazingly we had no flats or blowouts on the way there. It was now time to drive back to California and my uncle was pointing out to her that her tires were not in good shape for such a long a trip. He would have helped her get replacement tires, but WWII was still in progress and rubber was still a premium unattainable item.

With no way to get new or recapped tires, we left for California anyway on one rainy late summer morning. David had a learners permit and was driving up a hill in southern Minnesota when he lost control on the slick pavement and we spun out into a ditch. A farmer with a team of horses pulled us out. After that only my mom drove.

Early one morning after we left Laramie, Wyoming mother skidded on a downhill portion of the oiled highway. The right front wheel skidded into a low stump on the side of the road and the car rolled over. I think most of us passengers were asleep so we all woke with a shock at being upside down. I remember my grandmother saying, "Oh my, oh my, oh my!"

Being asleep we were all relaxed and aside from a few bumps no one was seriously hurt. No such thing as seat belts in those days. I was in the back seat with my grandmother and LeRoy. David was in front with my mom and the dog. I reached forward and turned off the ignition, fearing fire. Our dog, Mitze, had been sleeping on the passenger side floor and wound up tangled in the wires under the dashboard.

Shaken, we all rolled down windows and climbed out as a couple truck drivers going the opposite way stopped to help. Finding no one hurt they and some others who had stopped helped roll the car right side up. The right front knee action of our 1936 Chevrolet was completely bent out of shape so we needed a tow to the nearest town which was Sinclair, Wyoming. One of the drivers offered to send back a tow truck from Sinclair. In about an hour a tow truck came, but passed us by. We assumed he was going some place else and continued to wait. Another hour went by and then the tow truck that had passed us returned. He stopped this time. He had been told the car was upside-down, so when he saw our righted vehicle he assumed we had just stopped by the side of the road and passed us by.

The night before the accident my mom had met a couple from Minnesota at our motel in Laramie. While we were waiting for the tow truck at the side of the road, they drove by and seeing us stopped also stopped to see if we had a problem. They took some us in their car while my mom rode in the tow truck to Sinclair, where we waited in the only hotel in town to learn what it would take to fix the car. The bad news was we had a broken right front knee action and the garage would have to send to Denver for a new replacement. A knee action was Chevrolets 1936 answer to front coil springs. The car had a left and right knee action in place of front left and right coil springs. The hotel was too expensive for us, so we slept in a B&B the first night. My mother didn't like the conditions at the B&B. Our friends from Minnesota decided not to abandon us in Sinclair and returned the next day and drove us all about twenty miles to Rawlins where we found an inexpensive motel for another couple nights until the knee-action arrived and the car repaired. Our new friends stayed with us until the car was fixed ferrying us between Sinclair and Rawlins, until we were back on our way to California.

My mother courageously showed strength to us three kids and grandma after the accident and the remaining drive to California. She never drove at night. We always stopped before it got dark. When we got to San Bernardino it was late in the day and being only sixty miles from home she didn't want to spend another night in a motel, but mom was uncertain of driving in the dark to Long Beach. Remember these were the days before freeways. The roads were dark, unlit and most were just two lanes. So she called my Uncle Gene Brockway, Moms brother-in-law. He drove all the way to San Bernardino and we followed him home.

Mom had the 1936 Chevrolet repaired, but we never liked it after that for with a new right knee-action and a worn left hand side knee-action the car bounced with more gusto on the right side as it encountered bumps in the road. She sold it and bought a 1940 Chevrolet with an inherently bad clutch.

BOY SCOUT CAMP

I loved the Boy Scouts! For a boy without a father, it provided me with adult male associations that I found nowhere else. My two uncles that lived nearby never offered to take me or my brother on any outings, even though both often went on fishing and hunting trips. At least I thought they didn't at the time. Today I often wonder if their offers may have been blocked by my worrying and overly protecting mother. If an uncle wished to offer a nephew a fishing or hunting trip he would first have to ask his sister-in-law. A mother who had lost her husband and who was ever fearful of something happening to her sons, might easily decline such offers out of fear that something might happen or out of fear that she might lose control. Each year my Boy Scout troop made arrangements to go to the Long Beach Boy Scout camp at Idyllwild, California. The boys would spend the first part of a two week period in the scout park and then backpack up to Round Valley at about the 10,000 foot level in the San Jacinto Mountains. They would spend almost a week camping in the high country, hiking to a hidden lake and to the San Jacinto 11,500 foot peak. Each year I saved my money in anticipation of this wonderful event. And each year without fail, it just happened that our family vacation to Big Bear Lake always conflicted with the Boy Scout camp date. I was forced to choose between a family vacation with my mother and two younger brothers or the boy scouts. The family vacation logic and arguments always seemed to win out. I now wonder if I had chosen the scout camp on any of those occasions, if I would have been allowed to actually go.

On one occasion we had returned from our Big Bear vacation before the boy scouts returned from Idyllwild. My Uncle Gene Brockway was going to drive up on a Sunday morning to help drive some of the boys home. He invited me to come along with him. And again, something was scheduled so that it was inconvenient for me to go with my uncle. In retrospect my mother's manipulation was clever. She never actually forbade us to go to the Boy Scout camps, but something was always thrown into the planning that coaxed us to choose family activities or the family vacation. I always felt a loss in this area. It was something that I always wanted to do but for some reason I was never able to attain. I now find it amazing that I never suspected my mother of manipulating the situations. Of course I doubt that I knew the meaning of the word in those days. I also doubt if any of those Boy Scouts ever went back to Idyllwild as adults. But I have been drawn like a magnet to hike and to camp in those mountains with my children on five different occasions. After one has been through the manipulation process, it's amazing how easy it is to see it being exercised on and by others.

One of my mother's final attempts at control was after I returned from thirteen months in Korea. I was released from active duty in April 1953, and in July, the Saint Barnabas church Singles group were planning a cruise to Santa Catalina Island aboard a ninety foot schooner. My mother walked into my bedroom and said she felt the trip was dangerous and she didn't want me to go. I told her quite firmly I was twenty-three years old, I had just spent thirteen months in Korea in a combat zone, and I was going. That occurrence seemed to be the beginning of the end of her attempts at controlling her oldest son's behavior.

DANGEROUS ADVENTURES

On the northeast corner of Wardlow and Cherry in the 1940's was a sawmill with a wonderfully massive sawdust pile. It was great fun to jump and roll in the sawdust. It was even more fun to tunnel into the sawdust pile and make little rooms which we referred to as forts. When the workers would note what we were doing they would chase us away and collapse the tunnels. But as soon as they stopped watching we would come back and begin playing in the sawdust pile again. No matter how many times we were warned of the danger of getting suffocated, the attraction was just too great. It still amazes me that no one suffocated during those dangerous adventures.

Running east and west under 37th Street north of our home was a large forty-eight inch flood control drain. One time we took our flashlights and slid into the opening at the curb level--then slid down a two foot diameter pipe to the main drain which was about ten feet below the street level. Once in the main pipe we could walk for miles under the street. We were wise enough to only do this in the summer time when the pipes were dry. Although it was adventurous, it did get boring, in that walking slightly bent over for long distances wasn't very comfortable--besides when all you can see is a drain pipe running off in the darkness, we decided there was much more interesting adventure outside and came back to the surface.

THE 30-30 CLUB

The Long Beach Press Telegram Newspaper sponsored a night at the Long Beach YMCA for all newspaper boys in town, wherein we were allowed to swim in their pool, then see a movie, followed by a candy bar as we exited on our way home. My brother David and I regularly took the bus six miles from our home to downtown Long Beach on each Monday evening, walked several blocks to the YMCA, skinny dipped in the pool, saw a movie, received a candy bar and returned home. Relating this story years later people are surprised at the boys skinny dipping in a YMCA pool, but it was common practice in those days and we were not shocked about the procedure. Most of the boys didn't have suits with them and it eliminated carrying a wet swim suit home.

FOOLISH BOYS

I was thirteen years old, and we were visiting my uncle on his farm near Bowlus, Minnesota. My cousin Adrian was my age and we spent a lot of time together. One Sunday afternoon the families were visiting under shade trees out in the yard. My uncle had a .22 caliber pistol which fascinated me and I wanted my cousin to go gopher hunting with it. Adrian and I were up in a bedroom and he was showing me why he wasn't supposed to use it because it was malfunctioning occasionally when it was cocked. He was holding the pistol barrel parallel to his stomach trying to get it to stay cocked, when it malfunctioned and fired. The bullet creased his shirt leaving a tear and powder burns on

41

his shirt and stomach. His older brother Charlie heard the shot and called us to the window from the yard below and wanted to know if anything was wrong. We said no and immediately found another shirt for Adrian to wear. The experience sobered both of us and we decided to leave the pistol alone after that near tragedy. Young boys can be very curious and very foolish.

NEON SIGN TRANSFORMERS

Don Brown and I were experimental fourteen year olds. We procured some old Neon Sign transformers and hooked them up to a 110-power supply and danced a three to four inch spark between two wires. We insulated ourselves from being grounded by standing on a piece of wood. We hooked one wire to a metal base and wrapped the other around a stick of wood. Always respectful of the voltage involved we danced the spark over Sow bugs we placed on the metal plate.

My mother came out to see what I was doing one day and asked, "Isn't that kind of dangerous?"

I answered, "Oh no Mom, I'm well insulated by these pieces of wood."

It was very dangerous, even though the amperage was very low. But, fourteen year olds don't think anything will happen to them and that they are invulnerable!

BROTHER PHILIP'S EYE IN THE SKY

Initially we thought our first year algebra teacher in our all boys St. Anthony's High School had eyes in the back of his head. Whenever he was facing the blackboard, writing out the solution to a problem, he always knew just what was going on behind him in the classroom. Without looking around he would call out, "Johnson, sit back down!"

or "Miller, stop talking and pay attention up here!" It was uncanny, how did he know who was misbehaving?

Then one day about a month into the semester, one of the boys was helping to clean the blackboard and glanced up at a picture hanging just above the center of the blackboard and found the answer. The dark pastoral scene framed with clear glass made a perfect mirror the way it was propped at an angle.

Immediately the word went out! If one of us got into the classroom before Brother Philip, we would adjust the picture so it was hanging flat against the wall. As soon as our teacher began to write on the blackboard he would glance up and good naturedly comment, "Say... who's been messing with my picture?" Then he would reach up and prop it at the correct angle and we all knew we were again reflected in that eye in the sky.

BASEBALL BACKSTOP

I don't remember his name, but he was as short as I was in my freshman year of High School. He was short, but he had a gang. How words with him started I don't remember. All I recall now is that he called me out to meet him after school behind the baseball backstop in the school yard. Pinched between the backstop and a chain link fence was an area where two boys could fight without anyone seeing us from the school buildings. But an area that could be blocked at both ends by a gang. A place to fight with no way to escape or make a strategic withdrawal-I thought about this challenge all the rest of the day. I knew if I went out there by myself I couldn't depend on him being alone-most likely his whole gang would show up. He was a tough little guy. I might just get a black eye or two, but mostly I was afraid if I started to get the best of him his gang would jump on me. I couldn't win this fight no matter which way it came out. After school I shot out the opposite door of the school and ran to the bus stop. The next day he called me a coward, chicken and some other assorted names. I responded with the reason that I was not going to show up anyplace where his gang would be along. His gang went with him everyplace he went, so all his promises to meet me without them fell on deaf ears. After this non-encounter and a few days of hazing about my being a coward he got interested in bugging some other smaller kids. I've always been glad I did not show up that afternoon behind the baseball backstop. Sometimes it's just best to do nothing!

A SLAP BROTHER

During lunch period, my buddy and I were running in the halls of our parochial high school. This was an after hours detention offense if caught. As we rounded a corner there was Brother Adrian, who grabbed us both and said, "Running in the halls, what do you two want, a slap or detention?"

Without a moment's hesitation we both answered in unison, "A slap, Brother!"

For a brief stinging slap was far more palatable to two fourteen year olds than forty-five minutes of detention after school hours. Using both hands, Brother slapped us in unison hard on the cheeks and said, "Now get out in the yard where you belong."

We both answered, "Yes Brother," as we quickly exited into the school yard. Both pleased that we avoided that dreaded detention.

I don't recall that either of us ever told our parents, for in 1944, all our parents would have said was, "Well, sounds like you deserved that-next time obey the rules."

ICE CREAM IN BOWLUS, MINNESOTA

Fourteen year old cousin Adrian was driving slowly. Fifteen year old cousin Justus was lying across the right front fender of a nineteen-twenty era Graham directing a weak flashlight beam at the ditch at the right side of the dirt road. The old sedan had no working lights. The night was pitch black with over cast skies-no moon or stars shinning through. The few farm houses along the way cast no significant light out onto the dusty bumpy dirt road. Adrian kept the car centered on the road by watching Justus's hand signals from the front fender. Younger brother David and cousin Billy were in the back. It was a hot humid July night in 1945, as we five cousins drove down this traffic less road on our way to Bowlus, Minnesota, four miles distant. This was a highly secret high priority ice cream run, meaning we didn't have permission to go-especially in an unlicensed car with no lights.

We made it without incident to Bowlus, enjoyed our ice cream immensely, and headed back to my Uncle Butch's farm. About a quarter mile from the farm the weaken flashlight gave out. We missed the last turn and drove into a potato field. We all piled out of the car and in the total pitch blackness stumbled around the field trying to find the road. Eventually we found it about fifty yards away. Once back on the road, we slowly made our way to my Uncle's farm using the farm house lights as a lighthouse beacon.

Standing in the barnyard was nineteen year old cousin Charlie, questioning us as to where we had all been. "To Bowlus for ice cream," was our answer. Older cousin Charlie cautioned us that we were all in big trouble if Pa (Uncle Butch) found out. Fortunately He didn't and neither did our Mother.

The Second World War was still going on and all able bodied men and women were in the service of our country or working in priority industries. St. Anthony's Boys High School in Long Beach was in special need of janitors. We were taught by the Holy Cross brothers from Notre Dame and Brother Adrian was in charge of the schools janitorial needs. He decided to employ boys after school and weekends to clean up the school which entailed sweeping out the classrooms, cleaning the chalkboards, sweeping hallways and waxing the hallways on Saturdays. I learned at fifteen how to run an industrial waxer and buffer, which entails moving this heavy machine with select pressure on the handle to make it move effortlessly down a hallway from the left to the right side of the hallway. The pay was good for a teenager at that time. Unfortunately the school really wanted a full time Janitor and eventually found one after a year which put us part time janitors out of work.

CATALINA ISLAND BOY SCOUT CAMPOUT

It was 1946, and my brother David and I rejoined the Boy Scout Troop meeting at the St. Barnabas Church. The new scoutmaster was a test pilot for North American Aviation, and one of the assistant scoutmasters was a former Navy Frogman. For two boys without a father, both occupations really impressed us. A project was started collecting newspapers with the goal of getting enough money together to rent a water taxi to take the troop over to the isthmus Boy Scout camp on Catalina Island. I was sixteen and David was fourteen. My best friend, Don Brown, felt he was too old for the Boy Scouts and no longer belonged to the troop. His two younger brothers, Bernard and Leland, were still in the troop. I think once the work had been done, and the money collected, Don wished he had been a part of the whole project.

One summer Saturday morning we all met at a pier in Long Beach and boarded a sixty foot water taxi for the ride over to the island. As might be expected numerous boys got seasick going over.

Once we arrived, it was found that there was no pier and the water taxi operator would not beach his boat to allow us to get off. It was decided by the adult leaders that an available leaky rowboat could ferry the food and gear ashore. The men and boys would have to swim ashore. Our Frogman assistant Scout Master positioned himself half way between the boat and shore to help any of the boys that might need assistance. It was about a sixty yard swim and most of the boys had little or no trouble.

In those days, the whole isthmus was available for camping. The custodian in charge assigned our troop to the brow of a hill, just to the west of the isthmus. It didn't take long for us curious boys to discover that the east side of the hill had been an old Indian burial ground. We immediately began digging for skulls, bones and artifacts. The scout park custodian had to get our Scout Master to curtail our curiosity in this area for it was intended to be some university's future archeological dig when funds became available.

At one point, Johnny and I got into the leaky rowboat, and took turns rowing while the other bailed, as we attempted to explore the coastline. We saw a school of small fish right near the surface. Johnny decided to try and scoop up some for bait with a gunnysack. I held his legs and he leaned over the side. His head and shoulders were under water as he tried to scoop up a sack full of fish. When all of a sudden he pulled himself back into the boat yelling, "Shark, a big shark".

The school of fish were apparently on the surface in an attempt to elude the shark. We immediately rowed for shore where our Frogman assistant scout master grabbed a spear and he and another adult rowed out into the school, but by that time the shark had left and very quickly so did the school of fish.

After a usual Boy Scout dinner of half cooked food and an evening campfire songfest, we all got to sleep about midnight. About one A.M. the adult leaders came running through the camp with the custodian who was firing a carbine rifle yelling, "Wild boar! Wild boar!-follow us!"

They rousted us all up, and in various stages of dress with our trusty flashlights, we followed the custodian up a trail toward the middle of the isthmus. All of a sudden he stopped and yelled at us to point our lights into a large bush. There low to the ground was a wild boar, blood dripping from its mouth, beady eyes staring out at us. He immediately fired a whole clip into this awesome beast. Then he declared the boar dead even though those mean looking eyes were still staring out at us. He told one of us to crawl into the bush and to drag out the boar. Not one of us volunteered. After a few minutes of repeated requests and absolutely no volunteers, he crawled into the bush and pulled out a wild boar's head. Only then did we all realize we had been had! The boar had been killed earlier in the day and the adults had planted the head and fired the shots to give us boys a little nocturnal excitement.

As we boys followed our leaders back down the trail, we all decided that one good prank deserved another. As the Scout Master was walking near the beach we rushed him and threw him in the ocean. He was completely wet by the time the other adults realized what happen and came to his rescue. For the next three hours, the adult leaders systematically rounded up groups of boys, one and two at a time, and tying them together at the waist, marched them into the ocean. They were using a brand new rope which belonged to one of the assistant scout masters. At one point when they were marching a group toward the water, I rushed the group and in true heroic fashion cut the brand new rope and set a few boys free. I was then in real trouble, for I had cut a brand new expensive rope and the assistant scout master chased me and my brother David for over a mile down the beach. He caught David, but not me. They never did catch me, I stayed dry the whole night. About three-thirty A.M., when the majority of the boys had been dunked, we all finally went back to our sleeping bags.

The next morning after breakfast, we all boarded a war surplus landing barge which ferried us to Avalon where we attended Mass.

We were then taken back to the campsite, by the landing barge, and late in the afternoon the water taxi returned to pick us up. Again we had to swim out to the boat. And again the usual number were sea sick on the way back to the Long Beach water taxi landing. As our boat tied up to the dock, Don Brown, who had come down with his father to pick up his two younger brothers, jumped into the boat and said, "See, I'm in the boat, I went along too!"

I remember feeling sorry for him, for he missed out on a real great adventure.

MILLER! WHY DON'T YOU COME OUT FOR FOOTBALL

I graduated from High School in June 1948. One day in September 1948, as I stood watching the St. Anthony's football team practice on their field on Clark street in Lakewood, the coach walked up to me and said, "Miller, I've been watching you and you have filled out quite a bit this last year, how about coming out for football this year?"

For a short guy in his freshman year who had been waiting to hear this invitation for four years, I sighed and said, "Coach, I graduated last June."

THE END OF MY TEEN YEARS

I found myself musing one day on how many trips to Minnesota my mother made during my growing up years. She was very good about keeping in touch with her sisters and brother in Minnesota. My first recollection of a trip from the west coast to the mid-west was a train ride circa 1933. I have vague memories of riding in a Pullman car. The only reason I know it was about 1933, is that I have a picture of me at approximately three years of age holding up a fish someone had caught in the Mississippi, and prompted me to hold it as if I caught it. The reason I am so unhappy in the photograph, per my mother, was that I had not caught the fish, but was made to pose as if I had caught it and I didn't like holding that smelly old fish.

My next recollection is a circa 1936 car trip with Uncle Gene, Aunt Tracy, Aunt Hermina, my Mom, David, me, and cousins Glenn and Eugenia. We all sandwiched into Uncle Gene's new Hudson sedan. How four adults and four kids between four and eight years of age fit into that car including luggage, I'll never know. A continuing highlight on the trip was the passing of trains and us kids trying to couch the engineers into blowing their whistles. The adults tried to get us four kids to quiet down and nap, but invariably one of us would wake up upon hearing the steam engine and wake up the others and all four kids would actively try to get the engineers to blow their whistle. The actual visiting in Minnesota during this trip does not stand out in my memory for some reason.

I think the following incident at Aunt Della's farm happened either on the 1936 visit or on the 1941 visit. We arrived late at night and David and I were put to bed in an upstairs bedroom. In the morning I woke up all alone, in this strange bedroom. David had apparently awaken earlier and left me sleeping. I could hear voices coming up from down stairs. I opened a door and found a darken stairway leading down, but I was too afraid to go down into that dark void. I remember going back to bed and wanting to find my mother, but afraid to venture into that dark stairwell. Finally my mother came up to check on me and everybody laughed at me for being afraid to walk down a stairs. But I had never been in a house that had a door at the bottom of the stairwell and another door at the top of the stairs. I had never been in a house that was constructed for very cold winters where the stairwell doors were used to keep the heat downstairs by closing off the upstairs of the house during the day.

Our next visit was after my Dad died, and Uncle Butch came out to California in the spring of 1941 and helped drive my Mom and we three kids back to Minnesota. Most of this trip has been covered by the Chapter 2 story entitled, Summer on the Farm.

My last trip was circa 1945 or 1946, I don't remember exactly. Chapter 3 relates a night drive to Bowlus for ice cream and an incident with a .22 cal revolver that occurred during that trip. This mid forties trip stands out most clearly because I was older. My Mom made other trips, one in the late forties after my grandmother Burggraff or Aunt Hermina died and David and I stayed at home with my Dad's sister, Aunt Meta Muntz.

Trips in the fifties were made by my Mom, David and LeRoy, but I was either working or in the army by that time. My next trip was made approximately forty years later on June 28, 1985, when Dianne and I visited Minnesota and her birthplace in Wisconsin.

We visited the old LeDuc house in Chippewa Falls, where Dianne's Aunt Bernice LeDuc showed us around. We saw the parish church, cemetery, and other points of interest.

We stayed in Royalton, Minnesota with my cousin Charlie Burggraff, who took us to the old Burggraff farm which he initially inherited and subsequently sold by 1985. I showed Dianne the Two Rivers ruins of the old flour mill at the confluence of the Two Rivers and the Mississippi, where as teenagers on our 1946 visit we would sneak down to the mill pond late on a hot summers night for a cool dip and if we made too much noise we would be run off by Vernon Peck, the then current owner of the old mill house dam and surrounding property. The millpond spillway was dangerous and Vernon was concerned we would get hurt and sue him. Vernon Peck went on to make a fortune prospecting for Uranium in Utah. We visited North Prairie, the parish church, the one room school house which had been sold and converted to a residence and greater downtown Bowlus, all two blocks of it.

CHAPTER 4
Young Adulthood
(The 1950's)

THE TOWNE THEATER, THE
DRAFT AND COLLEGE

It was the fall of 1948 and I needed money. I was signed up at Long Beach City College with an engineering major. But an eighteen-year-old college freshman can't properly exist without wheels and spending money. So I got a part time usher job at the Towne Theater, located north of the intersection of Atlantic Avenue and San Antonio Road in North Long Beach. That was the first step-the second step was to improve on my wheels which consisted of a Whizzer Motorbike, which was a less than 10 horsepower motor mounted on a bicycle frame. You can't take a date out on a motorbike, and you couldn't ride on the freeway in those days with less than sixteen horsepower. I found a 1941 Plymouth business coupe in a used car lot on Atlantic Avenue that I could buy on time for $50.00 down and $25.00 a month, if my mother co-signed the loan for me.

Days became very busy thereafter, homework from the math, physics, chemistry, English, economics classes fought for time with long hours of standing in an auditorium at the Towne Theater and the social time required by a singles group at St Anthony's for high school graduates, notwithstanding the call of parties for young adults my age.

Some time after I started as an usher, I felt it would be easier to work behind the candy counter rather than continually walking up and down the auditorium aisles.

One night a young boy laid 10 Indian Head pennies on the counter to pay for a dime candy bar. I knew right away these pennies were probably from his parents' coin collection. I questioned him but he maintained the pennies belonged to him. I gave him his candy bar, but kept the pennies separate, expecting an irate parent to come in later trying to get his penny collection back. No one ever showed up. Probably his parents had so many coins in their collection they never missed these ten. Ushering, after you have seen the picture a couple times, becomes very boring.

After two years at LBCC and some weak grades, I tired of school and ushering and decided to go to work at the Neilsen Pump Division of the Oil Well Supply Company. My reasoning was that ushering took up too much time that I needed for homework. So if I worked a year, saved my money, I could finish up my Associate in Arts degree without working at night thus allowing more time for homework. After two years in college I realized I had to have adequate time for homework to graduate with an AA Degree and go on to a University. The only wrinkle was it was now 1950, the Korean War had just got very hot and so had the draft. I just might loose my college draft deferment during the time I was working and not going to school. None the less I decided to take my chances.

NEILSEN PUMP DIVISION OF OIL
WELL SUPPLY OF US STEEL CORP.

It was the summer of 1950, and I had decided to look for a job to earn money to continue my schooling at Long Beach City College. I went to a College Placement Office at LBCC and they sent me to a paint store in downtown Long Beach. The manager expressed interest in hiring me. He said I would have to wear a suit and tie and be prepared to wait on customers in the front of the store as well as work in the back stockroom moving supplies around, all the while presenting a well dressed appearance when dealing with customers in the front of the store. Up to this time in my life a suit and tie were for church on Sunday, not the type of dress worn in a dusty dirty stockroom. I was told the main office in San Francisco would have to approve my hiring and that he would call me if I got the job. Feeling this situation was very indefinite, I continued to look for a job. I was sent by LBCC to the Nielsen Pump Division on Cherry Avenue about a mile from home. They were looking for a salesman intern to work in their factory learning all the jobs involved in building their style of oil well pumps with the goal of moving the intern into a salesman job once he had learned all there was to know about their pump manufacturing and repair business. I took the job and about a month later the paint store manager called and informed me I was approved by their main office and I could come to work. The paint store manager was very upset when I informed him I took a job in an oil well pump manufacturing and repair facility. He was aghast that I would work in a place that made smelly oil well pumps. I worked in this smelly place for about seven months; in the factory inspection room checking machined parts, drove pump liners to heat treatment plants in South Central Los Angeles, around the Vernon area, drove to various oil fields picking up oil well pumps that were clogged with sand and had to be broken down and repaired and finally in the oil well pump assembly area. My favorite job was driving to a remote oil field, locating the derrick, picking up the pump and returning it to the factory.

Many of the repairmen showered and changed out of their smelly oil drenched in the factory prior to going home. Whereas, I drove the one mile home, stepped out of my pants which were so drenched with crude oil they would stand up alone leaning against the wall and went into the house to shower. My poor mother said I reeked of oil in those days I worked at the Nielsen Pump Division.

SOMETIMES YOU JUST SHOULDN'T ASK THE QUESTION

It was December of 1950, I was twenty years old and living at home. I was contemplating going back to college for the 1951 spring semester. I had already attended Long Beach City College for two years with a pre-engineering major; and then worked at the Nielsen Pump Division of Oil Well Supply Company from June of 1950 to December 1950 to earn and save some money. My one concern was when I might be drafted. I was reluctant to sign-up for the spring semester, buy all the books and fees and then receive a greeting from President Truman. So I went down to my local draft board and inquired as to when I might expect to be called up by the draft. The elderly lady disappeared into the back file room for a very long time and then reappeared.

She said, "Young man I want to thank you for coming in! You should have been drafted long before this, but your name was in the deceased file. You can expect to receive your draft notice in the next couple of months. Thank you again for inquiring."

Since that time and a subsequent thirteen months in Korea, I have often wondered if it would have been better not to have asked the question and then worried for years when the draft notice would arrive. I received a personal greeting from President Truman and I was drafted in March 1951.

CHAPTER 5
My Two Years in the Army – March 1951 - April 1953

REMINISCING 53 YEARS LATER

In March 1951, about 300 draftees were assigned to Company B, of the 63rd Infantry Regiment, at Fort Ord, California, for sixteen weeks of Infantry Basic Training.

Just before I was inducted, my Uncle Raymond took me aside at a family going away party and gave me some good advice.

"Don't volunteer for anything and do the best you can on the IQ and aptitude tests."

At the inductee center in Los Angeles I worked hard on the tests, while aware that some of the guys around me were really goofing off.

We all participated in a sixteen week Infantry Basic training. Most of us were eighteen to twenty years old and single. Unfortunately some were newly married and a couple guys were brand new fathers. Some mothers sent sizable gift packages of cheese, sausages, crackers, candy, etc...most of which were shared with buddies. Almost all of us made it through basic training. Some of the lucky ones like myself got good grades on the aptitude tests. Following our basic training a few were sent to non-commissioned officer's cadre school and a couple to Officer's

Candidate School. I and a couple of others were sent to a school in Baltimore. The remaining 280 plus buddies were sent to Korea. All of them were assigned to the same hill on the front line, Heart Break Ridge, from which only one of them survived. Now, so many years later I am continually reminded by recent wars and conflicts, just how blessed I have been. If I hadn't listened to my Uncle Raymond, and had a lesser score on those tests and if I hadn't been assigned to a Counter Intelligence School, I too may have found myself on Heart Break Ridge that fateful day in 1951.

THE FIRST WEEK IN THE ARMY

I was given no choice of what branch of service I preferred; I was in the army infantry, like it or not.

I was shown how to make a bed, issued uniforms, rifle, helmet, boots, towels, etc...

The greatest challenge was learning to cope with this new experience and environment. Keeping a low profile and never challenging or complaining about a direct order was requirement number one. If we were asked to memorize the twelve general orders for a guard on guard duty, I memorized the twelve orders. If you were ordered to recite one of the twelve orders, I shouted it out with all the volume I possessed.

Some guys just never seemed to learn, and were marginally performing all they were asked to do and in the end were always getting extra guard duty, KP and extra work details.

The biggest adjustment for me was coping with the teaching technique that taught to the lowest common denominator. All instruction is repeated and repeated until the slowest or dumbest soldier in the group has mastered the direction being given. Those who understood and mastered the instruction the first time must sit there bored stiff while the instruction is repeated over and over, until all in the room have learned the procedure.

Woe to the man that falls asleep, for all are remanded repeatedly to stay awake. Those that fall asleep are subjected to KP or other extra chores. Fighting sleep when one is bored hour after hour was one of my most difficult tasks.

JESSE

Jesse had the bunk next to me in basic training, right under a window. Jesse was a fresh air freak. Each night before hopping into bed, he raised the window all the way and then leaped under the covers-for Fort Ord in March can get real cold, a real damp chilling to the bone cold. All around pleaded with Jesse to close the window. He wouldn't close it even a little. If I or someone else closed it, he merely got out of bed, said nothing and opened the window again. After a week or two of closing it and Jesse getting out of bed and opening it we were all ready to give up. Each time we closed the window, Jesse waited until we were back in bed, then got up, opened the window and did his famous leap over the head board and slipped under his covers in one fluid motion.

One night, as usual, Jesse waited until after lights out when we were all in bed, opened the window and made his running leap under his covers to the sound of ripping sheets. We had short sheeted his bed. Jesse poked two round holes in his sheet as he made his famous leap under his covers. He didn't move, we didn't close the window and he slept that way all night. Nothing changed however, I almost got pneumonia as did others in the barracks.

Eventually we all gave up and Jesse got his way, the window stayed open all night. Why didn't we complain to the Sergeant? We did. He said it was our problem, solve it ourselves.

THE SHOWER

Within one week after arriving at Fort Ord, California, I easily decided the US Army wasn't my forte. One of the first things the Army tries to establish in your mind is that you belong to it twenty-four hours a day. This is a new concept for young men who are use to some free time after daily working hours. Weekend passes didn't begin until the sixth week of a sixteen week basic training. This fact of belonging to the Army was continually brought home by the drill sergeant calling out the entire barracks each and every time he wanted a couple of us for a detail. A detail could be KP in the mess hall, sorting equipment in the quarter masters building, some other duty in the orderly room, or policing up the company area by picking up trash, etc... These details could last a few minutes to a couple hours. We never knew when the whistle would blow and those wonderfully familiar words, "fall out, fall out, lets go, hubba, hubba!" We were all required to stop what ever we were doing and to fall out in front of the barracks on the company street. Everyone had to fall out even if they only needed one or two of us. To deliberately avoid these calls was an unwritten no-no, for it subjected your buddies to being picked for an unwanted detail without exposing yourself to the same chance of being selected. One time I was in the shower. I had just soaped up and the whistle blew. I knew that by the time I dried off and got dressed, I would be the last one out and I might be disciplined for being so slow. Excuses did little good. I knew the sergeant would look in the latrine, but not necessarily in the shower room. I also suspected that if it was a small detail they might not take roll call. I waited until all those in the latrine had left the room, then I turned off the water and stood back against the wall out of sight still completely nude and soaped up. I heard the footsteps of the sergeant come into the latrine and then leave. I don't know what my punishment would have been if he had looked into the shower more closely – possibly requiring me to fall out in my birthday suit of suds and most probably being picked for the needed detail. I could hear them out on the company street assigning certain men to details.

Then the men were quickly dismissed without a roll call. I waited a discreet minute or two as my buddies reentered the barracks. I turned the water back on and continued my shower.

One of my buddies stuck his head into the shower room and said, "Miller, how did you get undressed so quick and into the shower?"

I replied, "I'm just fast!"

He stared at me and said, "I don't think you fell-out for that last detail!"

I ignored him with concealed smile and went on with my shower.

SNEERING

Our Second Lieutenant was a brand new second lieutenant just out of a college ROTC program and assigned to our basic training company. He was not an experienced leader of men.

One day out in the field it was quite hot. I had rolled up both my sleeves a couple turns and unbuttoned my fatigue jacket collar. The Lieutenant sees me, chastises me for unbuttoning my sleeves and collar without permission and orders me to crawl on my belly up a powdery dusty trail made by army tanks for about a hundred yards. The dust was so fine it flowed in the top of my jacket and out the bottom. Needless to say I was then really hot and dirty. Up to then I hadn't been a fan of the lieutenant, but now I really disliked him. This day, I was hot! The day was very hot! I saw nothing wrong with rolling up my sleeves or unbuttoning my fatigue jacket collar. I forgot for a moment that everybody in uniform must look the same, all buttons buttoned. If the Lieutenant had merely ordered me to button up I would have obeyed. But crawling up the trail I felt was excessive punishment for such a minor offense. Even after fifty years this officer's response to a minor infraction was wholly excessive and unjustified.

The lieutenant had a habit of driving out to the boondocks in his bright yellow convertible, top down, for our training exercises and when the day of training was done he returned to the officer's club by car and we troops marched two to three miles back to our company area. One day the company was training for air attacks, whereby the troops would take defensive positions on a ridge, dig foxholes and then a light Piper Cub type plane would come over and bomb us with flour. All targets were fair game-if you got hit-you and everybody else would know it because you would be covered with flour. Now days some committee would fine this cruel and unusual punishment and pass another law. The plane was late and the company had already formed into to a column for the return march to the barracks. Our Lieutenant was standing by his beautiful bright yellow top down car as the late arriving light plane dived on the 300 man marching column. The sergeants ordered us to scatter and find cover. There were standing oaks on both sides of the road and the 300 men found excellent cover very fast. Only one remaining target of opportunity remained and the plane did a wing over and dived on the convertible to the cheers of 300 men and sergeants. At first a yelling lieutenant stood by his car waving his fist-then he got in and drove off. Unfortunately a moving target is hard to hit with a sack of flour, but a challenge none the less for the airmen. The company of 300 cheered the pilots on as the car and chasing plane roared out of sight.

Generally our sergeants and other cadre were reasonable men, asking no more than they were willing to give themselves.

I often wondered about the lieutenant, was he as unpopular leading men on the front lines as he was in Basic Training?

LUNCH ON HIGHWAY 101

It was a Saturday, the end of our sixth week of Basic Training, six of us were heading for the Los Angeles basin for our first weekend leave at home.

We stopped for lunch at a roadside hamburger stand near San Luis Obispo.

When it came time to pay for our order, and elderly gentleman stepped forward and offered to pay for our lunches. He said he was in the First World War and one time long ago a gentleman had bought him and his buddies a meal. So now it was his turn to pass on the favor he received so many years earlier. He asked us to allow him the privilege of buying us lunch and that we could pass this favor on someday when we saw a soldier in need of a meal. We all thanked him and accepted his hospitality. As I write this I recall that in the ensuing years, I have not been in a situation where I remembered to pass this favor on.

Passing on a gift isn't always as easy as it looks.

SOS

As mentioned above, our first leave came at our sixth week of Basic

Training. Six weeks are just long enough to develop an abiding dislike of Army food and a patent desire to visit home and have one of Mom's home cooked meals. Our first leave started at noon Saturday and ended Sunday night at 9 P.M. Hardly enough time to make a leisurely 300 mile drive to Long Beach and return by 9 P.M. the next day. After arrival home, I enjoyed a wonderful meal on Saturday night and immediately collapsed into bed.

Soldiers in Basic Training are perennially tired. On Sunday morning my mother said she just received a wonderful recipe from Aunt Meta. When she brought out this new culinary delight into the dining room I moaned for there she stood holding a large platter of SOS. She was confused by my reaction, for she thought it was real good. I then explained to her that creamed beef on toast is known in the army as shit on a shingle, which we had been receiving at least once or twice a week for the last sixteen weeks.

THE OBSTACLE COURSE

It was now May 1951, and I and about 300 other recruits were in the latter stages of our sixteen weeks of infantry basic training. We had been shown how to field strip a rifle, how to fire it on the range, how to march and run everywhere we went, how to fire and field strip the light and the heavy (water cooled) .30 caliber machine guns, how to aim and fire the 61mm mortar, how to fire the tank killing bazookas, how to throw hand grenades, how to fire a .45 caliber *grease-gun*, how to camp out in the boondocks and how to dig fox-holes. This day we were being trained at the obstacle course, where live ammunition was fired about a yard over our heads as we crawled for fifty yards under barbed wire and past pits where live explosives were detonated. If one crawled half way between the pits it slowed a person down, and if one took a short cut and crawled too close to the pits the explosive blast would blow you over on your back and cover you with dirt. Care was taken by the officers' in charge to ensure that we all kept our butts and heads down! The whole company had to crawl through the obstacle course in squad size groups (12 men) once during the day and once after dark. Needless to say the day was hot, dirty and very uncomfortable. Some of the more observant quickly learned how to minimize the discomfort by getting off of our stomachs a bit and crawling a little faster to get ahead of the slow pokes; and to keep as far away as we could from the explosive pits and thereby move through course as fast as possible. If one was showing too much of his posterior the cadre made him go back and do it again. In the darkness it was a different matter, you could get up on all fours and crawl as fast as you wanted to go, always keeping in mine that if you got your butt up too high you might get a .30 caliber machine gun round through it. About half way through the course at night, a buddy and I observed that two of the five machine guns would consistently overlap their tracer bullet fire and then swing their guns in the opposite direction. This consistent practice made a 20 yard wide swathe that was free of tracer bullets for about ten seconds.

I said, "Bobby, what do you think?"

In a moment we both agreed, and as the tracer swathe widen the next time, we both stood up and ran the last twenty yards. Leaping over the cadre and machine gunner at the end of the course, we kept on running disregarding orders to halt until we were lost among the other troops that had already finished the course. Of course the cadre sergeants and officer in charge just about had heart failure, stopped the firing of all the machine guns and immediately turned on powerful flood lights not knowing how many of their trainees were trying to run through the obstacle course or how many may have been shot. When they couldn't locate us and when they assured themselves that everyone else was on their stomachs they resumed the exercise.

In retrospect, foolish youth does and gets away with many a dangerous act, often solely to obtain a brief respite from a little discomfort.

A NEEDED SHOWER

Late in our sixteen weeks of basic training we had been in the boondocks for over a week and a half and we were all extremely dirty. The sergeant asked for volunteers to go back to the company barracks area to police it up and to make sure all the barracks were swept out prior to the company's return. The incentive to get volunteers was the promise of a shower before the clean-up detail returned to the boondocks. I volunteered! When we arrived at our barracks the group on our detail did not get right to work, so I decided I would get my shower reward first and then help them clean-up the barracks. I quickly showered, dressed in clean fatigues and then helped in the clean-up. Just as we all finished, the sergeant came back, saw that we were all done and ordered us back into the trucks for the return trip to the boondocks.

Morale to story, when in the Army, take your reward when you can get it, for rest assured the sergeant will always change his mind or the ground rules

A DARKEN BARRACKS ON A DARK STREET

One night in the spring of 1951, in the latter stages of our sixteen weeks of infantry basic training about a dozen of us were called outside and marched through the dark night to a not too well lit area of the fort where we were taken into a darkened barracks. In a partially lit corner of the building, we were told that the results of the IQ tests we had taken when inducted into the army would allow some of us to go to cadre or officer's candidate schools (OCS) and some to other army schools. This particular evening, representatives of the US Army's Counter Intelligence Corps (CIC) were looking for a few good men. We were asked if we would be interested in being assigned to a special school at Ft. Holabird, MD, after we completed basic training. The school would cover the mission of the Counter Intelligence Corps which was to contribute to the successful operation of the Army establishment through the detection of treason, sedition, subversive activity and disaffection, and to detection and prevention of enemy espionage and sabotage within the Army establishment or areas over which it may have jurisdiction.

We were all draftees and required to give the country twenty-four months of active duty and five years in the reserve following release from active duty. We were told that if we went to cadre school and then on to OCS we would be required to give Uncle Sam an additional year, which didn't seem too attractive since new 2nd Lieutenants at that time were being sent to Korea where the attrition rate for new officers was quite high. (As the new officers tried to get the draftees on the front lines to stand up and charge the enemy, North Koreans and Chinese, so as to lay down their lives for their country, the exposed lieutenants were getting shot by the enemy at an uncomfortably high rate.) We were told something about counter intelligence work and it all sounded quite attractive and adventurous to us twenty year olds. Especially since going into the CIC wouldn't extend our 24 month initial commitment. While coming out of the Army as an officer was attractive to me, the Korean attrition rate for young officers and the additional twelve months service was definitely not attractive. A couple of weeks before we completed basic training five of us were told we would be going to the CIC School at Fort Holabird, Baltimore, Maryland. We were told if anyone asked, we were to say we were going to the Signal Corps School at Fort Holabird.

Some of our basic training cadre were aware of where we were going and told us the old wives tale to worry us that once indoctrinated into the intelligence community you were in it for life.

FORT HOLABIRD MORNING ROLL CALL

It was August 1951. One of the most surprising things I experienced upon arriving at Fort Holabird was the immediate issuance of a permanent Class A pass.

In July, I had just completed sixteen weeks of basis training at Fort Ord, California. During basic training we only received a Class A pass on selected weekends and the pass had to be surrendered at the company Orderly Room upon return.

I was now to be a student for four months at the Counter Intelligence Corps Center, Fort Holabird. At the end of each weekday we were free to leave the Fort, but we had to appear at roll call each morning, Monday through Friday, and sometimes on Saturday. This was a whole new concept of Army life from the restrictions experienced in basic training. As one might expect, as the schooling became more routine, some of the men shaved their Monday morning returns to the Fort very closely. Even weekday roll calls became more and more difficult for the sleepy heads to make. Our designated barracks and class leader would cover for those absent by indicating we were, "All present and accounted for". When one or two were missing from an entire barracks lineup their absences were not visually apparent. Then as we marched off to class the slowpokes would join up with the marching column out of the bushes lining our route. As you might expect more and more men failed to make roll call especially on Monday mornings after a long week end. Our barracks leader who was a student just like us pleaded with the delinquents to mend their ways before we were all caught and disciplined. On one particular Monday, following a long holiday weekend, fifty percent of our barracks was missing from the roll call formation. As our barracks leader called out, "All present and accounted for", the first sergeant just happened to glance up. He did a double take and then directed our barracks leader to turn around again and look at the ranks behind him. Needless to say we were all in trouble, even the ones who were present and on time, for this is the Army's approach to discipline. All in Class B-115 immediately lost their Class A passes, the innocent and guilty alike. I guessed that the Army's thinking was that peer pressure from the innocent would straighten out the guilty. Although I did suspect the first sergeant wasn't quite sure who was there and who was missing so he just pulled everyone's pass, because some of the innocent had been covering for the guilty. However, within two weeks our passes were returned, and the roll call attendance was markedly improved thereafter.

Another aspect of life at Fort Holabird was the step up in the moral character of students at this school. Whereas in basic training at Fort Ord I had to keep all my valuables under lock and key, at Holabird, I could leave my wallet containing money laying on my cot while I took a shower downstairs and no one would bother it. The only thing we borrowed from each other was clothes, such as a sport jackets or with reservations a car. If one of my buddies had a date they would freely borrow my sport jacket if it was clear I wasn't going to use it. One of the students had a car. If he wasn't planning on using it a particular day or night, he would loan you his car. Your only expense would be the gas you used. Most of the students were graduate accountants or lawyers. There were a couple of engineering majors, myself and another man named Robert Miller. Why accountants and lawyers? Because accountants and lawyers are use to asking questions, which is just what the Army wanted in their investigative special agents. How we two engineering majors got into this organization I could never figure out.

SURVEILLANCE TRAINING

It was late fall 1951, I was near the end of my four months training at the Counter Intelligence Corps Center at Fort Holabird, Maryland. Today was a surveillance training exercise. A team would be chosen to tail a suspect and report in later where that individual went. A suspect, who was really a CIC Special Agent, was to be picked up in the main train station in Baltimore and followed. The idea was to follow the suspect without the suspect becoming aware that he is being followed. In the trade if the individual doing the following has been spotted by the suspect, he is burnt.

Our six man team rode to the pick up spot together in a government car with Maryland plates. All CIC Military Intelligence cars in those days had Maryland plates. Even if they were used in other eastern seaboard states, they all had Maryland plates-so much for secrecy. We put on our best suits and trench coats, for all special agents in 1951 wore trench coats, or so we believed.

We picked up or identified our suspect in the Baltimore's main train station. We all recognized him as one of our instructors during our months of training. While this made it easy to recognize the individual, we knew he was a expert, and that we had to do a real good job or we would be identified or burnt, which means he had picked us out as one of the individuals that were following him.

I picked up the suspect as did the rest of the team. I sat on a bench fifty feet from him reading a newspaper. For a while he also sat on a bench and then left and walked out of the terminal. He stood at a bus stop and then got on a bus going into downtown Baltimore.

One of our team got on the bus as the rest followed in our government car. He rode a number of blocks and then got off the bus. I was dropped off on an opposite corner. As I stood there our suspect was looking around trying to pick out who was following him. I just knew he was going to burn me as I stood back in the crowd as much as possible. A bus came at right angles to the suspect and I had the bright idea to get on it, ride a block, get off and return to the suspect's corner. I got on the bus, rode a block, certain that everyone on the bus knew what I was doing, got off and ran back to the suspect's corner only to find him gone. A bus had come, the suspect had gotten on, our government surveillance car had picked up the members of our team that were there and I was left alone. I had lost the suspect-I had lost my entire team-oh the embarrassment of it all!

I had an emergency number to call. I said, "This is Miller, I've lost the suspect and my entire team." The embarrassment of it all!

The voice at the other end of the line said go to a particular bar on East Baltimore Street, where they are all going to meet for a final critique of the exercise. I caught a taxi and went to the bar.

As I walked in the instructor was at a back table talking to our team indicating who he had burnt and what mistakes they had all made. He looked at me and said he did not burn me. I didn't have the courage to tell him that I had lost him miles back as well as the rest of my team. The embarrassment of it all!

OUR MISSION

The Mission of the US Army's Counter Intelligence Corps in 1951 was to contribute to the successful operation of the Army establishment through the detection of treason, sedition, subversive activity and disaffection, and to the detection and prevention of enemy espionage and sabotage within the army establishment or areas over which it had jurisdiction...

GRADUATION

After spending four months at Fort Holabird and graduating from Class B-115, I was promoted to a Private First Class and given a thirty day pass and orders to report early in January 1952 to Fort Lawton, Washington for assignment to the 441st CIC Detachment in Tokyo, Japan.

A month's leave at home was well appreciated.

Back in July 1951, following Basic Training at Fort Ord, California, I took the train as directed cross country via Chicago to Baltimore. A hot and grueling four days in a Pullman car. When we arrived at Fort Holabird we found out that we could have purchased a plane ticket and cashed in our train tickets and meal tickets after we arrived at Fort Holabird, thus avoiding that awful hot train ride. So on our way back across country in December 1951, I purchased a plane ticket from Baltimore to Washington DC National then to Chicago and on to LAX and avoided the long winter train ride. This was my first ride on a four-motored Lockheed Constellation cross-country. Flying in 1951 was long and arduous, and it was the first time I became aware of the harmonics that are set up by four engines not quite in synchronization. I learned years later that to smooth out the harmonics can put the plane out of trim and some pilots run the engines out of synchronization to avoid the trouble of battling the rudder trim tabs. To smooth out the imbalance can cause port or starboard engines to pull harder thus disturbing the aircraft's yaw trim.

Following a 30 day leave over December 1951 I flew to Seattle and Fort Lawton, boarded a General class troop transport in February 1952, and after three weeks of constant sea sickness arrived in Tokyo in March 1952 where I was immediately reassigned to a CIC Detachment in Seoul, Korea.

NOT A GOOD SAILOR

As I walked up the gangplank of the Marine Phoenix, a General type troopship in Seattle, Washington, that early February morning in 1952, I thought I don't belong here, I don't want to go to Korea, guys are getting killed over there.

Our Military Transportation Service ship was run by civilian merchant marine personnel.

The trip was fine for the first couple hours until we hit the mile long ground swells in the Straits of Juan de Fuca, where the ship slowly went up up up for a mile then down down down for a mile and I got seasick, and stayed sea sick for the next eighteen days. Thousands of men are stacked five high in the passenger holes of this ship, a great many of them in various stages of seasickness, throwing up in their steel helmets.

And I had picked a bottom bunk that on land is a prime choice location, but on a troop ship with five sick guys above you is a very very bad choice. What comes out, by gravity then comes down.

The ship's passenger holes after a few days reeked of sweat and vomit! So thousand of men opted to spend as much time on deck in the fresh air as possible. Our type of ship had enough fresh water for drinking and a very limited amount for bathing. So naturally the fresh water showers were only turned on for very short periods of time. The rest of the time we had to take salt water showers which after a while makes the skin sticky, discourages bathing and adds significantly to the rich ripe odor in the passenger holes.

About eight or nine of my classmates from Fort Holabird were on our ship. We generally congregated together on deck. One of our group volunteered as a mess steward for the civilian crew that ran the ship. They ate extremely well and this buddy of ours liked to eat and consequently ate very well as a steward. We were always encouraging him to bring us leftovers from the civilian crew mess which was separate from the troop mess. As we were lounging on deck, he would arrive with a covered large tray of leftover rolls and donuts from the crew breakfast. These always disappeared immediately for what our group couldn't eat there were thousands of other mouths to take them off our hands. The only problem was he didn't come out often enough.

One of the rules, enforced by the Military Police on board, was that if you vomited in the mess hall you had to clean up the mess you made. As I indicated, I was sick the whole eighteen days going to Japan. I was getting dehydrated and knew I had to get some food on my stomach. But to eat I had to stand in line on deck, then stand in line on the ladder ways going down a couple levels to the mess hall, then stand in a chow line, then try to eat something when nothing smelled good and all the odors were making me more nauseous. After a couple days I felt I just had to eat something. Well, I got all the way to the table with my chow, fighting nausea all the way. I took one look at the food, turned away from the table and threw up all over the floor, which sent the table I was at into convulsions and number of others threw up as I stood up and ran towards the door with two MPs right behind me yelling for me to stop. They wanted me to stop and come back and clean up the mess I made, but I knew if I didn't get some fresh air I would vomit again. I out distanced the MPs and mixed with the thousands of guys out on the deck. I guess the guys on KP (Kitchen Police) had to clean up the mess or some of the guys that threw up at the table after I started it all.

But I was sick and I just couldn't bring myself to voluntarily go back down into that mess hall with all those odors.

CIC VILLA AT CHUNGSUNGPO-RI, CHUNGSUNGPO-UP, TONGYONG-GUN, KYONGSAMNAM-DO

I arrived at Inchon, Korea in late March 1952, via a landing barge, for that port is shallow and couldn't take deep draft troop ships. It took us twelve hours to go as many miles by train to the Yongdungpo Replacement Depot outside Seoul. By noon of the next day most of troops from our ship had been assigned from the Repo-Depo to the front lines and I was getting worried that I might be sent to a front line Counter Intelligence Corps detachment. But then a couple of guys from the Seoul Counter Intelligence Corps Detachment arrived in a commandeered Russian truck and drove us to a hotel in the city. A couple days later we were sent by train south to Pusan assigned to the 704th CIC Detachment.

At the 704th CIC headquarters in a nice plush tourist hotel outside Pusan we new arrivals were told that the sub-detachment on Koje-do Island needed additional personnel. The executive officer, a Major, told us that it had been the practice to send all their misfits to the island as a form of punishment. He said the accommodations were very poor at present but should improve when the sub-detachment moved into new quarters just outside the POW Camp. He apologized, but said some of us would simply have to go over to the island. He handed us some dice and said the four individuals that rolled the lowest numbers would have to go to Koje-do. I rolled snake eyes.

Koje-do Island is twenty miles south of Pusan, Korea. It is a cloverleaf shaped bit of real estate about fifteen miles on its longest leg. In 1952, it was the site of United Nations Prisoner of War Camp

Number 1, which incarcerated about 200,000 Chinese and North Korean Prisoners of War (POWs).

When General Douglas MacArthur made his famous Inchon landing and cut Korea in half a year earlier, our Army captured almost over night a quarter million Chinese and North Korean POWs. The UN POW Camp No.1 was set up in a big hurry. Groups of five thousand POWs were placed in very large virtually unmanageable compounds which they controlled more than we did. We kept the POWs in by threatening to shoot them if they tried to escaped-but what they did in the compounds was pretty much at the will and direction of their Communist leaders and officers.

The humanitarians through the Swiss Red Cross insisted the POWs be given shovels, rakes, saws, etc to build things and to grow vegetables. More often than not the tools were made into weapons and used during riots and breakouts to kill UN soldiers. (The liberal appeasement mentality was beginning to start in the 1950's) The POWs communicated between compounds using signal flags, kites bearing messages, and the POW dispensary/hospital where they met prisoners from other compounds. Escape tunnels were being dug all the time in many of the compounds.

The indigenous ferryboat to Koje-do was only about 60 feet long with two decks. The open top deck was reserved for the crew, pilot house and VIP personnel, namely us, whereas the lower deck was jammed with all the Koreans traveling to the island. The very cold and damp trip took about three hours. We curiously watched the deck below as a food vendors sold dried fish and squid to the travelers-much as a states-side vendor would sell popcorn or peanuts at a ballgame.

We learned later that this form of travel was not an approved method of military transportation. The military ferry was a small (Mr. Roberts) style cargo ship that took all day and stopped at other coastal ports along the way. Once on the island the military ferry docked at the main POW camp port of entry and we would have had to be driven nine miles across the island to our quarters. Also the island G-2 used the port of entry to keep track of who was being assigned to the local CIC detachment because we didn't report to him directly, but to a higher G-2 at the Korean Communications Zone (K COM Z) located in Taegu.

As we on our indigenous ferry approached one of the largest towns on the island, Chungsungpo-ri, we saw one lone jeep waiting on a stone jetty. We soon learned that the driver was a corporal, a cook, who was in charge of the sub-detachment kitchen. It seems the actual cooks were two Koreans who had cooked for Japanese generals in WW II. He said he restricted his job to just picking up the rations at the POW camp main quartermaster depot and letting the Korean cooks have free reign in preparing the meals. Apple pie was one of their specialties.

As he drove us to the compound located on a bay about three miles north, he filled us in on the real facts concerning this sole CIC sub-detachment on Koje-do Island. The POW camp was located nine miles to the west over two small mountain ranges.

It seems that the Korean owner of one-third of the island, in a patriotic gesture of cooperation and friendship, had volunteered his villa on this beautiful bay north of Chungsungpo-ri, to the CIC sub-detachment-presumably for a couple months while their permanent quarters were being built. Unfortunately, it had now been over a year, the man wanted his villa back and the CIC sub-detachment was stalling, refusing to move out with the excuse that their quarters just were not completed. The owner had appealed to numerous authorities, but getting this military intelligence unit to move was difficult. The corporal suggested that the real reason was that the sub-detachment officers didn't want to move out of these plush quarters, but we could make up our own minds when we arrived.

As our jeep entered a lush valley, about a mile away on the beach rose a high stone walled compound that looked initially like a medieval fortress. Within the compound was a large stone two story building at its northern end and the roofs of a quadrangle of buildings on its southern side.

The corporal explained that the upper story of the stone building were our offices, and the lower story remained the owner's warehouse. Around a fountain were arranged the quadrangle of Japanese style buildings, which we used for the detachment sleeping quarters, bathrooms and dinning room. The owner had been camped out on the beach for the last year in a group of cabana style buildings and he was getting very tired of the arrangement. One very important point was made, headquarters in Pusan knew nothing of this arrangement or the posh style of quarters that allowed each officer his own private room with enlisted personnel no more that two or three to a room.

We asked how could this arrangement go on for a year without someone getting wise? Simple was the answer, someone from the island sub-detachment would always go to Pusan for the monthly payroll and to pick up the PX liquor ration at the same time. Correspondence that couldn't be mailed were always hand carried or picked up by island sub-detachment personnel, who magnanimously volunteered to make the cold wet journey to Pusan, rather than subject someone from headquarters to the damp voyage by military ferry and an uncomfortable night stay in our cramped and poor quarters. If anyone from CIC headquarters in Pusan did come over to the island, MPs at the island port-of-entry always gave us a heads-up, and arrangements were made to put them up in the BOQ at the POW camp rather than subject them to the torturous nine mile ride over two mountain ranges to our humble compound.

Shortly after our arrival, one of our two master-sergeants asked me if I wanted to ride shot-gun to Chungsungpo-ri where he was going to do some trading. He didn't bother to explain to me that he was going to sell a number of cartons of cigarettes on the local village Black Market. It was a pitch black night as he stopped the jeep in a dark alley. The sergeant had placed about a half a dozen cartons of cigarettes between us as he was negotiating with someone on the left side of the vehicle. I tried to peer around him to see what was going on. As both of us were distracted, someone on the right side of the jeep reached behind the two of us and stole all six cartons without either of us noticing. The sergeant blamed me for not being more observant. While I realized I had been very naive, I felt if he had bothered to let me know just what he was up to and just what kind of characters he was dealing with, I might have been more cautious and more help. Of course as a PFC, you don't say that to a master sergeant.

When the officer-in-charge found out I could type, he assigned me to the office as his clerk. Once a day we had to call the CIC headquarters in Pusan via army field phones. Army field phones of that day were notorious for their low volume especially over long distances. The officer-in-charge was a man with a raspy voice with minimal volume, so he usually asked me to initiate the call. Yelling at the top of my lungs I would eventually work myself through various Army field telephone exchanges until I got in touch with our headquarters in Pusan. It occurred to me often that it might be a lot easier to open the office window and yell across the twenty miles of ocean rather than try to get through on an Army field phone.

One day our badges and credentials arrived from Fort Holibird in Baltimore. The badge was a two and a quarter inch bronze detective like shield with Department of the Army across the top and Military Intelligence across the bottom, accompanied by a credential that reflected we were Special Agents in the Department of the Army's Counter Intelligence Corps and all military personnel were enjoined to cooperate with us. Not ordered to cooperate mind you, just enjoined. How does a PFC enjoin a commissioned officer to cooperate? Very simple, don't wear PFC stripes, but put on officer US insignia on your collars and pass yourself off as a Department of the Army civilian. When interviewing an officer, flash your badge and credential, and if asked what your rank is simply state you are a civilian.

One morning a buddy and I were walking up the driveway of POW Camp #10 in Pusan, where I had been temporarily assigned for a month, when a staff car pulled up behind us and honked its horn. We moved over a little, to let it by but apparently not enough. The driver honked again and we moved over again, and he honked a third time at us before coming to a stop. Out came a captain and a one star general. The captain called for us to stop! As I and my buddy turned around to meet them the captain looked at the US's on our collars and asked for identification. "Who are you people?"

I answered, "Department of the Army civilians, Sir!"

The captain glared and the general sputtered, "Well the least you could do is get out of the way of my car!"

I answered, "Yes Sir".

The captain glared at us with a non-believing look and held that look as the general strolled off calling for the captain to follow him. My buddy was in a cold sweat, as he accused me of having more guts than brains.

"Miller, you just lied to a general", he whispered.

My feeling was I never did like parading around in officer US's acting like someone I'm not, but if I'm expected to do it to accomplish my job, then I would play out the act all the way. One of the reasons our civilian charade worked so easily was that the Korean War was labeled as a United Nations Police Action and UN civilians, Swiss Red Cross, American Red Cross were all wandering around the POW camps ensuring that the POWs weren't mistreated-generally being a pain in the neck to the military authorities. When we flashed our Department of the Army badges and credentials, seldom were we challenged. The badge was a bronze two and a quarter inch shield with Department of the Army across the top and Military Intelligence across the bottom of the shield. I always thought it was a good-looking badge.

We ate in the POW Camp #10's Officers Mess. We signed in like all the other officers, doctors, nurses and civilians. One day at lunch, I walked in with a couple other Special Agents, signed in and dropped my pen. Bending over to pick up my pen my .38 caliber snub nose detective special revolver dropped out of my shoulder holster from underneath my jacket onto the floor. I had forgotten to snap a hold down strap in place. Civilians were not supposed to be armed. I quickly picked it up and returned it to my shoulder holster. A couple of nurses standing nearby stared at me with a questioning look but didn't say anything. Civilians were not to be armed. As I said, we were seldom if ever challenged.

Once on Koje-do Island, one of my buddies was challenged by an officer in charge of a BOQ (Bachelor Officers Quarters) at a remote southern military site on the island. As a counter intelligence organization, we periodically inspected remote military sites to ensure compliance with the handling of classified materials and to review any incidents connected with treason, sedition, subversive activity, disaffection, espionage and sabotage. It was a day's drive over very poor single lane rut like roads to this site and the special agent, a PFC like myself, wore officers US insignia and opted to stay over night in the site BOQ. The officer in charge of the site BOQ was suspicious and called our Koje-do Sub-detachment officer in charge, a captain, and requested the rank of the special agent. Our officer in charge stated, if he was a military person, the agent couldn't be more than a major because the commanding officer of the 704th CIC Detachment in Pusan was a major and this agent did not out rank his CO. The site BOQ officer decided not to pursue the issue any further and the agent henceforth spent the nights of his periodic visits in the site BOQ.

My mechanical aptitude also got me assigned as the detachment projectionist. We were scheduled to receive a couple movies each week. A way of increasing the number was to trade movies with other units. A couple nights each week, I would show our movie early and then quickly drive back to the POW camp and trade our movie with a

Military Police detachment. I then returned to our detachment and we had a second late show that night.

The road between the POW camp and our villa was a single lane rut about nine miles long, over two small mountain ranges. The route was very dark, isolated and patrolled only once each evening by the Military Police. The road passed through one village that had reported in the previous weeks that live stock had been killed by a large panther like animal. Returning one April evening with a movie I was bundled up real good against the cold. Underneath a pile vest and field jacket I was armed with only a .38 caliber two inch snub-nose revolver. As I passed a village farm, moving only about 25 mph, a very large black panther ran across the road and jumped up on a low bluff over looking the area of road that I was about to pass under. Stomping on the brakes I fumbled under my layers of clothing for my revolver. The vehicle almost skidded to a stop under the bluff when I decided trying to pull out a revolver, which probably wouldn't do me that much good anyway, was a waste of time. I quickly concluded immediate movement was the better part of valor and stomped on the gas pedal while expecting the panther to land in my lap any second as I accelerated the jeep past the bluff. Needless to say for a long while thereafter my pistol was in my hand as I drove past that particular spot in the road, especially at night.

Evenings were boring and after a few drinks the men occupying one of the rooms decided to rid their room of rats. When they saw one crawling along a rafter above their heads they would pull out their .45 automatics and start blasting away. The holes they put in their tile roof came back to haunt them the next time it rained.

In another section of our Japanese style villa with an enclosed overhead-one night someone got the idea of activating and then throwing a whole bunch of insecticide spray cans into the enclosed overhead to drive out the rats above their room. The next morning the Captain in the next room had rat shit all over his bed, pillow, table and his candy bars had been gnawed into by all of the rats driven out of the overhead next door.

This villa was heated by building fires under the clay floors of the rooms and allowing the heated smoke to flow up vents between the walls. The walls between some of the rooms were just a thick layer of paper. One night during a bad dream I rolled right through my wall and landed in the lap of a Chinese Captain reading in his bed in the room next door. In today's mentality the place was a fire hazard.

Many military units would often let young boys from the local villages hang around their units. Ours was no exception. Danny O'Yoon, a seven year old, was our unit's mascot, mainly because he was befriended by one of our sergeants. One day Danny was poking around the room I shared with our cook, when Danny pulls the cook's revolver out of his holster hanging on a chair, points the gun at the cook and pulls the trigger. Both of us grabbed at the boy at the same time, but neither of us reached him in time to prevent the hammer from falling on the chamber. Fortunately, the cook kept the next chamber to rotate up empty, and we got the gun away from the boy before he could pull the trigger a second time. When we told his sergeant benefactor about the incident, we both got bawled out for allowing him to get near the revolver. He told the cook to keep it out of reach in the future. In today's world seven year olds would not be allowed to wander freely around a military installation, especially a military intelligence organization.

This pleasant logistics arrangement continued for another three months until the Pusan 704th CIC headquarters adjutant, (the Major we met on our arrival) decided to make an unannounced inspection tour of outlying sub-detachments and turned up one day unexpectedly. He said, "You SOBs, you had us all believing you were living and working in a hell hole!"

Needless to say the sub-detachment's officer-in-charge was transferred, and then we were all moved immediately into the POW camp into half wood half stone buildings over looking a hot dusty motor pool which had a very bad habit of starting its diesel trucks about 5 AM each morning. Then for the next two hours on the half hour it was, "Two and a half ton drivers, start your engines." Then, 30 minutes later, "three quarter ton drivers, start your engines." Many a morning I fantasized climbing up the pole to the loud speakers and cutting the wire.

One day around noon, a truck drove up to one of the POW compounds with a load of sand which had been requested to fill in low spots and mud puddles in the compound. The POWs mistakenly thought the bags were rice and took them to the compound kitchen. The compound leaders started a riot after opening the bags, saying the Americans were now trying to starve them and trying to feed them sand. The riot was just getting started when the food truck arrived with the daily ration of rice.

The POWs used any and all reasons to demonstrate against the ones is power. Sounds a little like our politicians of today!

By the summer of 1952, the conditions in UN POW Camp # 1 were becoming so bad and uncontrollable that the UN authorities knew they had to break up the 5,000 man compounds and put the prisoners in smaller more controllable pens. This situation was brought to a head when the Commanding General was pulled into a compound one afternoon and held for ransom by the POWs. The mistake the general made was to go to the compound to talk to the leaders, instead of making the leaders of the compound come to him in his office. When a Honey Bucket detail, returning from the bay after dumping raw human waste, was passing through the compound Sally Port type entrance, they dropped their Honey Buckets and grabbed the general and pulled him into this 5,000 man compound. The general was finally released after signing a document admitting certain actions the POWs had been complaining about. The large 5,000 man compounds were then split up into much smaller more manageable 500 man compounds late in the summer of 1952.

KOREA

I spent thirteen months in Korea, first as a Special Agent assigned to the 704th CIC Koje-do island Sub-Detachment in UN POW Camp No.1, for a short time at Pusan's UN POW Camp #10 and later in Taegu at the 704th CIC HQ. Only during the last two months of my assignments in Korea was I assigned field work which in my case was conducting background investigations of Korean nationals applying for jobs in Army establishments.

Very boring!

I did go out on a security inspection one time wherein an inspection was made of an entire unit as to how they were handling classified data. Do they lock up secret data properly, do they control the log-in and log-out of classified data according to military procedures, etc...?

So much for James Bond type intelligence work. However, I must admit, in my entire stay in Korea, I never even heard of a special agent really doing any cloak and dagger type operations, not that I was necessarily aware of all the classified work that was going on. Operations were on a need to know basis, if you needed to know about something you were told about it, if you didn't have a need to know you were not suppose to know or inquire. Therefore, to sum up my Special Agent activities in the Counter Intelligence Corps of the United States Army, I would classify my stay as-very boring.

THE LIAISON PARTY

It was the late spring of 1952, our Counter Intelligence Corp (CIC) Detachment was invited to a South Korean National Police liaison party in a small village hotel about ten miles from our beautiful bay side billet. We sat on the floor on mats at a long table, Japanese style. Each of the Korean National Police and/or ROK Army Intelligence attendees individually went around the table toasting each of the Americans with a small cup of Sake. We were then expected to return the toast. All was going well and I felt the potency of Sake was somewhat overrated for I didn't feel it was having much effect on me. After an hour and a number of rounds of toasting I had to go to the restroom. While in the bathroom the Sake hit me. They laid me down in one of the small rooms in the hotel. I remember getting sick. As I lay on a mat on the floor, I saw a monster crawling towards me. As I raised up, focused and took a closer look, I realized the creature was a cockroach. I immediately threw a glass of water at it and laid back down and went to sleep. Later in the afternoon, my friends came and woke me and said the party was over and it was time to get into the jeeps and to return to our compound. They helped me into the passenger side of a jeep and our two vehicle convoy started out, our jeep in the lead. My driver kept telling me to keep an eye on Cap, the driver of the second jeep. He kept repeating, "Keep an eye on Cap! Cap's drunk, but I'm OK, I'm sober!" Even in my fuzzy state of mind, I questioned the sobriety of my driver. The ten mile stretch of single lane cliffhanging dirt road led across two mountains ranges, often following the coast two or three hundred feet above the beach. Within the first mile or two the journey became a race between the two drivers, each trying to maintain the lead. To this day I'm still uncertain how those two managed to repeatedly pass one another on that one lane cliffhanging road. Very quickly my head started to clear as I hung on hoping that I'd survive the ride. As we raced into the motor pool of our compound, they all poured out of the jeeps yelling it was time for another drink! As I just sat in the jeep, digesting the fact that I'd survive the ride, our executive officer walked up and asked, "Are you all right?" I just nodded and slowly got out of the Jeep, stone sober, but with a twenty-two year old's brand new appreciation of the potency of Sake.

A LITTLE NIGHT VISITOR

Our sub-detachment, in the east valley of UN POW Camp No. 1 was billeted in long half stone half wooden buildings located on one of the hillsides above the POW compounds. One dark early morning I heard scratching at an inside door to my bedroom. My half awake awareness immediately assumed it was another one of the many huge rats that we had been unable to eradicate. This particular creature seemed bent on getting into my room. It finally pushed through a screened air vent in the lower part of an inside door and proceeded to cross the room toward an outside door. The outside door fit snugly and it couldn't squeeze through to the outside. At this point I raised up on my army cot to get a better look and this little beast heard my movements and began to walk slowly toward my cot. I reached under my pillow for my flashlight and revolver. My movements made the cot squeak louder and this four-legged shadow started to trot toward me. In half asleep fumbling motions I tried to point my flashlight and cock the pistol. I let out a yell as this incredibly aggressive animal put its two front paws up on my cot and emitted a low, "Woof". It was only then that I remembered that the day before some buddies had brought back a puppy. With my heart still wildly pounding I ushered this little night visitor out of my room, while assuring my buddy in the next room that my yell was only caused by a bad dream.

JEEPS DON'T GET STUCK

I was 21 years old, in the Army, in Korea on Koje-do Island at UN POW Camp No. 1, and I had an unfailing faith in that renowned military vehicle, the Jeep. I had grown up during the Second World War hearing of the wonderful accomplishments of this vehicle in the South Pacific, Asia, Europe and Africa. In my opinion the Jeep could go anywhere. One afternoon I decided to avoid a dusty drive behind lumbering army trucks by taking a little used road over a small mountain which appeared on the map to be something of a short cut to the next valley. All was going well until I came upon a very large mud puddle. I didn't know how deep the puddle was, but not to worry, a Jeep could conquer all. I got a running start and I expected to blast right through that puddle. About halfway through I came to a wrenching stop with my transmission balanced on top of a very large submerged rock. All four wheels were under water, but not touching anything. I then quickly learned that Jeeps can get stuck, especially when none of the wheels can get any traction. I spent the next hour carrying rocks to the puddle and filling up the holes under each wheel. Apparently a stuck army truck had dug some very deep holes in that particular puddle. The motor pool sergeant was not too happy when I brought back a very muddy vehicle-but the driver was much wiser.

TIME TO GO HOME

One day in March 1953, I was called into the commanding officer's office in Taegu. He reminded me it was time to end my time in the service and to be sent home. He had been calling all of us draftees into his office during the last few days and encouraging us to reenlist for another year. He offered to make me a corporal, a one step increase in rank, if I would give him another year. I politely declined stating I wanted to go back to school. Actually about half a dozen of us PFC's, all Special Agents, were due to rotate home for release from active duty at the same time. We had discussed amongst ourselves the pros and cons of such an offer. Our biggest compliant was that we had given this detachment a year of our lives and not one of us were promoted during that year. Our Table-of-Organization allowed for more sergeants and corporals, but this commanding officer was reluctant it seemed to promote draftees. We had all agreed that another year out of our lives was not compensation for a one step promotion to corporal. We all declined his offer and were sent home.

The army trained us for a year, sent us half way around the world, and this major thought it was too much to give out a few promotions to retain that experience.

Actually if he had offered me sergeant stripes I would have enlisted for another year. As it was I came home, met my wife and these vignettes tell the story.

MY FIVE YEAR ARMY RESERVE REQUIREMENT

The draft law of the early 1950's required a draftee to spend two years on active duty and five years in the reserve, either in an organized reserve unit which could be activated as an entire unit or in the ready reserve which allowed for the army to call you back on active duty as an individual. After I was released from active duty in April 1953, I was offered a chance to join the Los Angeles Counter Intelligence Corps Detachment assigned to the Los Angeles basin. I was eager to get back in college and civilian life. I chose the ready reserve, which didn't require me to go to any meetings. Later I regretted my decision for not joining an organized reserve unit which would have given me extra money as I raised a young family, a chance for an extra retirement and the work might have developed into something quite interesting as the country moved through the cold war years. The only negative that might have occurred would have been that a reserve unit might have been activated into the Vietnam War.

One of those life decisions that I'll never know what would have been better!

Department of the Army Military Intelligence (CIC) badge

1951-Fort Holabird Honor Guard

1952-Roger standing outside quarters on
Koje-do Island, South Korea

1952-Roger eating ice cream at UN POW Camp
#1, on Koje-do Island, South Korea

1950-Troop Ferry to Korea, U.S.NAVAL
SHIP MARINE PHOENIX

CHAPTER 6

My Twenties After Two Years of Active Duty in the Army

(The 1950's)

MASTER LAYOUT DRAFTSMAN TO WORK PACKAGE MGR

Following is a brief summary of my jobs from when I got out of the army to my retirement in February 1994. I was released from active duty in April 1953, and promptly got a job at the Long Beach Douglas plant as a Master Layout Draftsman. Master Layout (MLO) is the flat pattern development of sheet metal part layouts which are then used to fabricate form block tooling, router block tooling, drill templates, punching templates, stretch form die templates, etc… It was an hourly paying job which didn't pay that much per hour. The layouts were drawn to plus or minus .005 of an inch which required the extensive use of a magnifying glass. I worked at this job for about five months until I went back to LBCC in the Fall of 1953.

In a very short time I found going to school on the GI Bill didn't give me enough money to satisfy my needs and I took a part time job during the Fall of 1953 and Spring 1954 semesters at a small Mom and Pop market at Wardlow Road and Walnut Avenue, called Howard's Market.

My intention was to work at Howard's Market during my remaining two years at Cal-State Long Beach.

After our marriage and Dianne announcing she was pregnant with Deborah, in the Fall of 1954, I went back to Douglas and requested my MLO job back. It seems they were always short of experienced MLO draftsmen. The job required draftsman skills, keen eyesight and an extensive background in Trigonometry and sheet metal fabrication techniques; but as I mentioned before, it didn't pay that well, so they always had people looking and leaving for better paying jobs.

After about four years, I found a Project Engineering salaried position at North American Aviation in Downey in 1957. The Navaho Program was in full Research and Development and NAA was hiring. My Project Engineering job was to describe and document engineering design changes that went into contract change proposals to the Air Force Contracting Officer. Nine months later the Navaho Program was cancelled by the US Air Force and I was laid off; my one and only layoff in my working career. I hunted for a job for three weeks and then reluctantly returned to Douglas' MLO department. I worked there for nine months.

Following my June 1958, graduation from Cal State University at Long Beach with a BA in Business Administration, I again went looking for a better paying position. I found an engineering management position at Hughes Aircraft in Fullerton, where I worked for four years from 1958 to 1962, monitoring costs and schedules on selected Radar programs.

In 1962 the Apollo space program was really getting started and North American Aviation was again hiring. I got an Engineering Planning position which entailed monitoring costs and schedules for a

Flight Technology Department which was a whole new field devoted to calculating navigation in space from the earth to the moon and back. Nine months later I was promoted to Supervisor in Engineering Planning where I supervised engineering planners in numerous engineering departments. In 1965, I was promoted to Chief (a junior manager position) over about one hundred twenty-five people in an Engineer Data Management Department. Data Management received, filed and disseminated all technical data coming into the engineering departments from suppliers and subcontractors working for us on the Apollo Program; as well as coordinated the assembly and transmittal of all contractual data to the NASA and other customer agencies and launch sites. In the early 1970's, I transferred to the procurement department where as a Major Subcontract Administrator and Work Package Manager, I spent the last twenty years of my career. Major subcontract management entailed the negotiation and administration of subcontracts over ten million dollars. At one period in the early 1980's, I was administering approximately two hundred million dollars of various open contracts with Hughes Space and Communication in El Segundo.

North American Aviation merged with Rockwell Standard in the late 60's, then became Rockwell International in the early 70's, and finally Rockwell Space and Communication Division was purchased by Boeing in the early 90's; after I retired. Consequently, I am now a Boeing retiree, while never having actually worked for Boeing.

MEETING DI

It was June 25, 1953, and into our Couriers singles group meeting walked this tall lovely girl. She introduced herself as Dianne LeDuc. I immediately decided she was the most beautiful girl in the room.

We were meeting in the St. Barnabas Church hall. I was twenty-three years old, newly elected president of the club, just back from

Korea and recently released from active Army duty. All the guys decided that, as the newly elected President of this singles club, it was my sworn duty to check this girl out and find out all the important particulars. I asked her to dance and proceeded to learn that she just recently graduated from high school in Portland, Oregon and moved down to Long Beach. She was engaged to a Marine at Camp Pendleton and was board and rooming with her aunt and uncle in the parish. I reported back to the other guys in the room that, worst of luck, she was engaged.

I had already come to the conclusion that all the really good looking girls get snatched up by the guys real quick. Here I was twenty-three years old and all the girls that I found attractive, even those in the club, were spoken for.

After the meeting that evening, we showed Dianne around Long Beach, especially the pike.

The summer of 1953, was lots of fun. The group had beach parties until the wee hours of the morning, and a weekend trip to the mountains where the guys slept downstairs and the girls upstairs, and a wonderful trip to Catalina Island on a chartered ninety foot three mast schooner. The boys slept in sleeping bags on the deck, while the girls slept below in the staterooms and lounge. Dianne and her Marine fiancé accompanied the group on a number of outings, including the schooner trip to Catalina.

As far as I know none of the singles in the club were sleeping together.

When the summer ended, I signed up for classes at Long Beach City College and for an evening biology class at Poly High School. A girl named Cathy, and Dianne signed up for a short hand class at the same high school. At break time, I and the girls would meet and talk. After school we would stop at the Clock Drive-in for coffee and pie.

I recall one evening as I was walking across a patio at the school to meet the two girls, I saw Dianne from afar and thought, now that girl would make a good wife.

Later at the drive-in I was sitting in the back of Cathy's car and noticed Dianne's engagement ring was not on her left finger. She told me she had broken her engagement. Within the week, in the latter part of October, 1953, I asked her to go to a movie. By January, 1954, we were engaged and on June 19, 1954, we were married.

TO MY HONEY

In mid-fifty-three, I met my honey,
in those days I did not have much money,

But to enhance the ways of our dating,
when I sure needed help with my rating,

I would pick her up at her employer,
and drive us both to a quiet corner,

Amongst the oil well pumps on Signal Hill,
from a bag would come a favorite pill.

She surely loved crème chocolate éclairs,
and these gifts really helped me put on airs.

This was before cholesterol and fat,
put us on guard as to where we are at.

Although that last line tries to be funny,
I'm still much in love with my honey.

DELIVERING THE US MAIL

In December 1953, using my veteran status, I obtained a part time job with the US Post Office to deliver mail. I was assigned to the Bixby Knolls Post Office which was close to home. My initial instructions were to meet a regular mailman on his route in the California Heights area where he would train and instruct me on mail delivery. I met up with the carrier. He handed me a wad of mail and told me to walk up one side of the block and come back on the opposite side of the street stating there is nothing to this job, "All you have to do is to be able to read numbers."

"I said OK," and proceeded to walk up the street delivering the mail.

When I got back to him, he said, "You are indoctrinated, go back to the Post Office and tell them you are trained and ready to deliver the mail."

They assigned me to a carrier, who took me out to his route, explained how the mail was cased and the route I should walk to deliver the mail. The first thing I learned was to not stick my fingers too far through the door mail slot for some houses have dogs that try very hard to chew the end of your fingers off. Second, all dogs have a hatred of all US Mail carriers. Third, if any Christmas tips are offered, they belong to the regular carrier. Fourth, if the dog won't let you near the mail box, that family's mail doesn't get delivered that day.

One fenced yard had its mail box hanging on the outside of a low three foot high white picket fence enclosing the front of the property right up to the sidewalk. A very protective large dog was in the yard. The dog would not leave the yard or jump the fence, but it would straddle the mail box with its front paws and defy me to put the mail in the box. An elderly lady in the house would watch me through a window trying to place the mail in the box without doing anything to control her dog. I would stand on the sidewalk waving a handful of mail, but she would make no effort to come out and receive their mail. I asked the regular carrier what he does when he can't get the mail into the box and he said he just wouldn't deliver it that day. I finally found that I would drive by this house again at the end of the day in my car on the way home and if the dog wasn't out in the yard I would slip the mail in the box. Rain, shine, storms, earthquakes, nothing deters the mail carrier from his appointed rounds, not even snarling dogs!

Usually the mail was so heavy at Christmas time that we would make two deliveries a day. The regular carrier would case the mail early, I would pick it up at the Post Office, and make a morning delivery. After lunch the carrier would bring more mail out and place it in the Swing Boxes, where I would pick it up and deliver the route again. If any interesting magazines were in the morning mail, I would save them and look them over at lunch time and deliver them in the afternoon.

JUST WATCH HER

We had been married less than a year when another couple, Dianne and I stopped in a LA hotel bar for a drink. I was twenty-three and the other couple were both over twenty-one. Trouble was, Dianne was just nineteen. The waiter carded us all and said Dianne would have to leave the bar because she was not of age. We explained that she was my wife, and she was only going to order a coke. The waiter said she would still have to leave the bar, but the rest of us could stay. We objected and he finally agreed to talk to his manager and left us for a few moments. When he came back he said Dianne would still have to leave. He said minors are only allowed in the bar when accompanied by their parents who can be responsible for them. We asked him to check with his manager, if a husband can be responsible for his minor wife. He again checked with his boss and said, if we agreed to watch her and be responsible for her, she could stay.

WATER AND ELECTRICITY DON'T MIX

My friend Ed, a co-worker at the Douglas Aircraft in Long Beach, came home one evening in 1953 to the unhappy news that his wife's car battery was dead. He went out to the driveway to see if he could possibly start the engine and recharge the battery. As he removed the battery caps, he noticed that the battery water was extremely low and a portion of the plates in each cell were exposed. Disgusted, he returned to the house and asked his wife if she ever had the gas station attendants check the battery.

She said, "Of course."

He then asked if they ever put water in the battery and she answered, "Well they certainly tried a number of times, but I wouldn't let them. Everyone knows that water and electricity don't mix."

HOWARD'S MARKET

Upon release from active duty in the Army in 1953, I registered again at Long Beach City College, forsaking my previous engineering major and signing up for an accounting major. I obtained a part time job at a mom and pop market at Wardlow and Walnut Avenue. Howard's Market was run by the owner. A mild mannered senior gentleman who insisted upon plastering all the front windows with so many ads that they blocked the view from the street. The police warned Howard that this made the store particularly vulnerable to robberies. And of course Howard was robbed numerous times, but he insisted in using his total front window space for advertisements. He had no safe and after closing at night he stashed his receipts under the baloney in the meat counter, or someplace in the store like behind the cereal boxes. Even though he always picked a different spot each night he always remembered where he had hid the money. I predicted that one day a customer was going to pull out a bag of sugar and expose a wad of cash.

One day Howard instructed me to particularly watch a seven year old named Susie. This little lady would come in and stand at the candy counter for a long period and then leave. Once as Susie was leaving Howard said, "Susie, stop right there, and empty your pockets!" Out on the floor dropped about a half dozen candy bars. During the length of time I worked in the market I never did actually see Susie take anything. One day as Susie was leaving after having spent about fifteen minutes standing in front of the candy counter, I was suspicious and stopped ringing up a customer and said, "Stop right there Susie, and lets have it all!" At which point she reached down with both hands and pulled her elastic pants out away from her legs and out dropped six candy bars. Leaving the candy laying on the floor she quietly left the store. Although Howard had talked to her mother many times, parental oversight was minimal and nothing seemed to change Susie. Howard was too gentle a person to push the matter any further. I've often wondered what happen to little Susie.

KIDNAPPED BRIDE

"Honey!" cried my brand new bride from across the hall.

As I turned around I saw her being carried horizontally out the door. As I raced over and out of the St. Barnabas Hall I was met by two football line backer sized guys who lifted me off the ground and held me in the air as my wife was driven off. We hadn't had our wedding pictures taken yet in church and I was pretty sure they would bring her back in a few minutes if I didn't try chasing them-so I just sat down and had a cup of coffee and waited. Sure enough they brought her back in about ten minutes.

After our small reception of punch, coffee and cake, Dianne changed out of her wedding gown at her Aunt Jeanne's house which at that time was less than a mile away. Then her stepfather, Art Moore, drove us to downtown Long Beach to get my car which I had stashed the previous day in an underground hotel parking garage.

The reason for all this intrigue was that I and my buddies had a tradition of playing tricks on one another during wedding receptions. My cousin Glenn Brockway stole his best friend Bobby Gillette's luggage out of his car, hung all of Bobby's bride's lingerie in his room and filled their suitcases with rocks. The couple didn't discover the switch until they got to their motel in Bakersfield. The bride's father had to drive their luggage to them after he finally found out that Glenn had taken it. Later, when Glenn married, I had gotten into his apartment during his wedding reception and took his luggage and later cancelled all of their reservations up the coast of California. So with the tricks I had played or been a party too, I was wary of what these guys would do to me. I definitely had something coming.

Dianne and I had packed completely the day before and I had hidden my 1951 Ford Sedan in a hotel parking garage on Ocean Avenue in downtown Long Beach. Art Moore was driving us to my car and we were being followed by a number of cars with my buddies and relatives who just weren't going to let me and my bride escape quite so easy.

Having grown up in the Long Beach California vicinity, I knew the lay of the land. As Art Moore drove down Pine Avenue and slowed for a stop light opposite the Desmond's Department store, my new bride and I jumped out and ran into the store. Our pursuers were taken by surprise. Once in the store Dianne and I headed for the basement to a little used pedestrian tunnel that led two city blocks to an underground shopping area under one of the hotels. Those following just weren't quick enough and thought we would run in one door and out another door of the department store. We lost them immediately. Once under the first hotel south of Ocean Avenue we exited into an alley and walked and half ran the remaining two blocks to the hotel where I had hidden my car. We were now safe and as we drove west on Ocean Avenue to

Highway 101 we passed and waved to one car of our pursuers still looking for us but going in the wrong direction.

We got to Santa Barbara in mid-afternoon and decided to keep going for a while longer. We ended up around 6 P.M. in Santa Maria and checked into a motel room. After such a hectic day I told my brand new bride I was ready for bed, but she said no bed until she was fed. So we had dinner which I felt took longer than it needed too.

CAL STATE UNIVERSITY SIDE WALKS

I was impressed. The Cal State University at Long Beach sidewalks lead right to where the students want to go.

It was the fall of 1954, my first semester at California State University at Long Beach. The permanent buildings were just being built. As the buildings were completed and occupied, the students beat paths between the buildings as their class assignments dictated. Just a few paved sidewalks were poured. Some were used, but mostly dirt paths as determined by the student body carried the young people from building to building. Then a most intelligent things happen, the dirt paths were paved over, for these represented the shortest distance between two points as decided by hundreds of students over a semester period.

As I would walk between buildings I marveled at the efficiency of their placement.

Years later, visits to other universities, corporate and government office complexes, show by their placement when a walkway has been located by a functional user or the eye of a designer. When taking classes at Cal State Fullerton I was amazed at how many students cut across lawns as they moved between their classes, proving some designer laid out the sidewalks, not the students.

NEW FATHER

As I held the back screen door open to our one bedroom apartment and allowed my wife, our brand new baby daughter and mother-in-law to enter, a frightening thought exploded in my brain, "I don't know how to be a father."

We had been in the apartment less than an hour, when the new mother and the new grandmother decided brand new baby Deborah needed a bath. Of course we had the latest canvas baby bathtub on the market. The two ladies propped up the latest *How to Bathe Baby* book and proceeded to wash the small creature. Step-by-step they lifted first one arm, then read the instructions, then the second arm, etc. When the water became cool, they warmed it up. Occasionally I would peek in and comment that the baby's skin was wrinkling up like a prune, but nothing discouraged the maternal drive of the new mother and grandmother. Then I realized that while I didn't know much about how to be a father, the new mother and grandmother sure didn't know much about bathing this small creature. Fortunately, time can be a great teacher. The little lady long ago grew into a lovely mother herself and both myself and Dianne learned how to be parents of three other lovely daughters and two handsome sons.

OUT SMARTING THE LITTLE LADY

We lived in a one bedroom apartment when our first born arrived. Our bed and the baby crib were in the same room. When we woke up the new baby woke up, and wanted immediate attention. At first we solved the problem by hanging a sheet over the crib side so the baby couldn't see us get up and leave the room for a quiet breakfast before changing and feeding her. At about six months, she learned to pull back the sheet and watch us. As soon as we stirred or showed in any way we were awake, she wanted immediate attention.

Our next trick went as follows: As I awoke, I would open one eye and look at Dianne who would wink at me and indicate the baby at the moment was not peeking around the sheet looking at us. I would very quietly slide out of the bed on the opposite side of the crib. Dianne would do the same. We would both then slide on our stomachs across the hardwood floor room, out the door and into the front room. Whereupon we would quietly fix breakfast and read the paper before attending to that demanding little egocentric creature in the crib. This technique worked until she was able to stand up and move around the crib. Then she learned how to spot us sliding across the room floor and we were forced to get her up also.

LOST KEYS

My keys were lost! We had given the keys to the baby to keep her quiet and now they couldn't be found. We looked everywhere. There are only so many places to put things in a one bedroom apartment and only so many places one can look. We pondered what to do? Then I got an idea, on all fours, holding my head off the floor at the height of a crawling baby, I crawled all over that apartment looking and feeling and touching anything the baby could see or reach. As I crawled along our short hallway, hanging on the door knob was the baby's diaper bag, a place a baby could reach. I stopped and reached into the unzipped bag and found the lost keys.

If you want to solve a mystery, sometimes you have to see and reach like the perpetrator.

IF DADDY LIKES IT, EVERYBODY LIKES IT

When our six children were growing up Dianne and I made an effort to expose them to a wide variety of different foods. In order to get them to try new preparations I had a saying at the supper table, "If daddy likes it, everybody likes it!" I would then try a fork full of the new cuisine and declare, "Daddy likes it". With this statement all resistance was to cease and they were expected to try a forkful or two of the new preparation. Occasionally their response was accompanied by some moans. One evening Dianne failed to drain the oil from the tuna can before she added it to a casserole. The resulting dish had too much oily liquid and it was not at all tasty. I arrived late to the supper table. The kids had already sampled the entree and were watching me intently. I sat down and tried a fork full. It didn't taste very good and I stopped eating. Immediately six pairs of hands pushed their plates away and one of the older ones said, "If daddy doesn't like it, nobody likes it!"

I went into the kitchen, got a loaf of bread, the jam and peanut butter jars and returned to the table where we all enjoyed something we all liked.

LOOK ME IN THE EYES

"Look me in the eyes, Dennis. Are you listening to Mommy? Look me in the eyes! Do not ride your bike in the street. Do not ride your bike into the street!" charged Dianne as she tried to instill into two-year-old Dennis the danger of riding his tricycle into the street. "Do you understand Mommy?"

"Yes Mommy," would always be his response. He would then mount his little tricycle and ride it down our asphalt driveway and right out into the street. She would yell and rush down the driveway, out into Dilworth Street, turn him around and usher him back onto our driveway admonishing him for his noncompliance.

Looking him in the eyes, getting his undivided attention, cautioning him was to no avail. Even though this scenario was repeated many times a day for over a year or two, fortunately he was never hit by a car!

I WANT MY BREAKFAST FIRST

Our oldest son Dennis had chronic Tonsillitis when he was a toddler and the doctor recommended he have them out. We took him to the Whittier Community Hospital the evening before the Tonsillectomy. They woke him early the next morning and took him into surgery. Of course, they gave him nothing to eat. When he recovered from the operation, they asked him if he would like some lunch. He said, "Yes! I want my breakfast first, then my lunch."

GUNKING A 51 FORD'S CARBURETOR

In the mid 50's I was working as a Master Layout Draftsman for Douglas Aircraft in Long Beach, California. A co-worker, Don, had a gunking solution which I borrowed to clean out my 51 Ford carburetor. After a day of soaking, I extracted the pieces and reassembled my carburetor. Over a period of time, I tried to adjust the carburetor with no luck. In desperation I asked my Uncle Gene Brockway to help me. After working on my car he said it was very strange but my carburetor was missing one of its jets. I was mystified for I thought I had reassembled it properly. About six months later my friend Don gunked his pickup truck carburetor and he said he couldn't figure out what to do with what appeared to be an extra jet. I told him to throw it away. Then I explained the gunking of my 51 Ford.

RUBBER CHECKS

The man from A-1 Equipment Rentals wanted to speak to Roger J. Miller.

I said, "Speaking."

He said, "Mr. Miller, your check of $60.00 written last weekend bounced."

I said, "Hold the phone while I look in my check book." I had done business with this equipment rental firm in the past, but I couldn't remember writing a check to them in the last week. I came back to the phone and said, "I didn't write a check for $60.00 this last weekend."

He then asked what bank I banked at and I said, "Security First National." He indicated the check he had was written on that same bank.

The conversation went downhill from that point. He insisted I was the Roger J. Miller that wrote the check that bounced. He asked me what the J. stood for in my middle name and I said, "Joseph." He then asked me what the J. stood for in the other Roger J. Miller's name and I said, "I have no idea." He then berated me saying, if he lived in a town where a man had the same name and used the same bank as him, he would most certainly know what the man's middle name was.

After further discussion back and forth, he said he'd leave this conversation as status quo, and he would talk to me later. I said, "No, you won't leave this as status quo, and I don't want to hear from you again."

A while later, upon receipt of my monthly bank statement and cancelled checks, in my envelope was a check that was not mine. It had not been charged to my account, it just appeared to have been filed wrong. I went to the bank, asked for a clerk and proceeded to tell this young lady that I had received a canceled check with my statement that was not mine. She looked at my name and this other guy's check and proceeded to argue with me that it was my check. I said "Look lady, it has a different return address." She argued and refused to accept back the check. So I asked to speak to the Operations Officer. I again explained the whole issue and he also argued with me that it was my check.

At this point I was just about loosing it! I said if he didn't want the check, and I didn't want a check that wasn't mine or part of my records,

I was going to tear it up in little bitty pieces and throw it in a sand filled ash tray next to me. I said, "I am now proceeding to begin tearing up this check!"

The Operations Officer said, "Don't tear it up sir, the other man may want it!"

I gave it to him, walked over to a teller's window and closed all my accounts in the La Mirada branch of Security First National Bank.

A VERY SMALL CONNOISSEUR

We gave our twenty-one month old daughter Debbie some play dough for Christmas. Dianne left her for a few minutes playing at the kitchen table. When she returned the play dough was all gone, and a small amount was dripping from the corner of Debbie's mouth. We looked everywhere for the remaining play dough. Concerned that she may have eaten some or all of it, we called our family doctor. He suggested we look on the container to see what were its ingredients. The label indicated it was non-toxic. We were advised to watch her carefully and if she appeared to become ill, to go immediately to the hospital. Days passed and she appeared to be fine. About a week later, Dianne decided to broil some hamburger patties and opened the oven broiler. Neatly placed on the broiler tray waiting to be broiled, were six patties composed of all of the missing quantity of play dough. Apparently Debbie had tasted a little and had decided they would taste better broiled.

CHAPTER 7
My Thirties
(The 1960's)

CARS AND ROCKS

I came home from work one evening to find the upstairs children's toilet clogged up. Dianne said she thought our four year old youngest son Daniel probably had something to do with the problem. As I worked a plumber's *snake* into the toilet, I asked my son what he had thrown into it. He answered very clearly, "Oh, cars and rocks!"

I looked up not wanting to believe what I had just heard, and said, "Now Daddy's not going to get mad, just tell Daddy the truth, what did you throw down the toilet?"

He again calmly answered, "Cars and rocks!"

At that point I abandoned the short plumber's *snake*, and rented a large motorized router and attacked the cars and rocks via the roof vent pipe. Eventually the motorized router ground up the cars and rocks sufficiently to loosen up the clogged sewer line. But every now and then over the ensuing years that particular sewer line sometimes still acts like a freeway parking lot.

SIX TIMES?

Explaining the facts of life come to all parents, some in humorous ways. During an explanation to Debbie when she was a very young girl, Dianne explained that the procedure whereby babies are made. When she was done, an incredulous daughter questioned, "Do you mean you and Dad did it six times?"

HIYA TORO

I, Paul, the Scout Master, and Roy, had walked our back packing troop of twenty Boy Scouts four miles into the Anza Borrego desert east of San Diego for a weekend campout. It was late in the afternoon when we arrived at our campsite near one of the few natural springs in the area. The spring had been tapped by the rangers so that water flowed out of a pipe into a watering trough for animals. The over flow just drained off into the desert sand. As the boys paired off and began to set up their tube tents, a wild steer with very respectable horns approached the watering trough. When the boys saw the steer all of their Matador genes collectively kicked in all at once and as a group they waved towels, blankets and red bandanna's yelling, "Hiya Toro! Hiya Toro!" At first the steer was startled, but its thirst won out as it lowered its head and continued to approach the watering trough. We three adults immediately yelled at the top of our lungs to try to get the boys to back off and let the animal drink. To no avail! Twenty boys yelling, "Hiya Toro," cannot easily be shouted down. The animal pawed the ground, lowered its head and charged the closest group of blanket waving boys. We three adults almost had simultaneous heart attacks. As the charging steer came near the boys they nimbly jumped behind scrubs and brush. We three adults were shouting ourselves hoarse, still to no avail. As the animal charged past one group of scouts, others behind it would yell, "Hiya Toro, Toro!" The beast charged over and over again, at no time did it ever come close to one of the nimble boys. Finally, we three adults just stopped yelling and watched as our twenty out of control boy scouts harassed this rapidly tiring animal. The poor steer never did get his drink, but finally retreated over yonder hill with twenty yelling scouts in pursuit.

Moral, even a charging wild steer is no match for the awesome energy produced by twenty yelling Boy Scouts. The steer never had a chance.

YELLOWSTONE NATIONAL PARK

Our family arrived in the afternoon at Yellowstone National Park and proceeded to search for an unoccupied camp site for our Nimrod tent trailer. Finding a nice site we settled in. Just before dusk a Ranger drove through the campground warning all campers that a grizzly bear had been frequenting this area at night. Everyone was directed to place all food stuffs in the trunk of their cars and to leave nothing edible outside or in your tent. Visibly apprehensive, we removed everything with any odor from the tent trailer and tightly locked it in our station wagon. For at the end of our campsite near the lake was a large steel culvert mounted on a trailer with a gate that would trip closed after an animal took the bait inside.

Around 2 AM we were awaken by someone beating on a frying pan and yelling. As I peered out the window a magnificent grizzly bear stopped next to our trailer door and proceeded to beat and pull the lid off a cooler after which it devoured the fish inside. A camper in back of our campsite had not heeded the Park Ranger's warning and left freshly caught fish out on a table in a cooler. As the foolish owner of the cooler approached beating on a frying pan, the bear grabbed a final mouthful of fish and retreated past the front of our trailer across the road into the woods. Retrieving his now useless and empty cooler, the unhappy camper returned to his camp site.

Another neighbor came out of his camper next to us to check on his two sons who were still soundly asleep in a pup tent. We exchanged a couple of excited comments about the tremendous size of the bear, when he abruptly turned and sprinted back to his camper vehicle. My first thought was, what a rude departure, until I saw the returning bear which must have decided a second course of fish was in order. I yelled to the owner of the cooler, "Look out! Here it comes again!" After much clamor and the beating of more pots and pans, the visiting behemoth was driven off a second time, only after I suspect it found the cooler empty.

Following visits to our trailer commode by most of our family and a firm commitment to the younger children that Daddy was definitely not going to bring the bear back so they could see it, we all tried to get back to sleep. Needless to say with the amount of adrenalin in my system, I laid in bed for the next two hours listening to each and every sound in the night. Finally I hear what I was waiting for from a long way down the campground, Bear! Bear! and the faint sound of beaten pans. I immediately rolled over and finally fell asleep knowing our hungry bear was occupied elsewhere dining on some other camper's carelessly stored food.

The next morning we mutually all agreed to fold up the tent trailer and leave for the Oregon coast. Our departure was relatively uneventful if you don't count the left trailer wheel lug bolts all working loose before we left the park. The whole wheel and tire would have fallen off if it was not contained by the trailer wheel well which held it in place until we were able to stop. I had heard a strange noise from the trailer and asked Dennis to stick his head out of the rear Station Wagon window. He did and said a scrapping noise was coming from the trailer. We stopped and discovered all the lug bolts had come off but were contained by the wheel hub cap.

I learned then and there that a four lug wheel that is of a small diameter and consequently turns at a high RPM just has to have its lug bolts especially tight, for they have a tendency to work loose more so than a car's five bolt configuration.

The two younger children were also happy when they were able to see a mother black bear and two cubs grubbing for worms in a rotting log.

EARLY MORNING ON HIGHWAY 101

I was driving north alone on US 101 near Paso Robles, California at 6 A.M. when I came around a bend and saw a VW bus with an obvious flat tire. The vehicle was surrounded by five very disheveled looking young men with a sixth figure lying beside the bus. They flagged me down and I brought my station wagon to a stop about a hundred feet beyond their vehicle. I thought to myself, I'm taking off if they all run up to my wagon, but if one comes up, I'll talk to him. One young man did run up and said they had a flat tire-they had a jack but no lug wrench. He said they had been sitting there for over four hours and no one would stop. I thought, no wonder, the way you guys look! I had two 4-way lug wrenches in my trunk. So I backed up, but still a little apprehensive about getting out amongst this disheveled group. As I got one lug wrench out of the wagon I imagined them hitting me with it and taking off with my car and money. As they used my wrench to change their tire, I stood by trying to think of an excuse to quickly leave. Then I looked at their spare tire and said, "That spare looks as bad as the tire you're taking off. I've got another lug wrench in my vehicle, so keep this one because you'll probably have another flat soon enough". I then headed for my wagon and they all followed me, even the one that had been sleeping beside the bus.

They all began thanking me profusely, wishing me flowery blessing and a beautiful day. As I drove off, I thought, Wow! Looks sure can be deceiving.

GEORGE AND ALICE

We belonged to a church group of half a dozen couples that met twice a month to discuss scriptural subjects and family issues.

About six weeks before the holidays one year, I sent each of the couples in the group a Christmas card from a George and Alice, a fictitious couple. I mentioned different personal occurrences in each of the cards that had happened at church or social gatherings that would be recognized by each of the addressees. I also included a promise that George, Alice and family would be dropping by their home from out of town during the holiday season.

At our next gathering, one of the men asked, "Who are George and Alice? I don't remember meeting them." Others mentioned that they too had received a card and they too couldn't remember meeting this couple.

When a dozen people could not recall a George and Alice, it then became obvious that someone in the group was perpetrating a practical joke. Handwriting samples were collected from each member of the group and then for the rest of the evening all joined in trying to discover who was the practical joker. No one ever guessed who sent the cards.

CHAPTER 8
My Forties
(The 1970's)

SEVENTY-TWO OYSTERS

There were seventeen of us! We had five of our six children and Chuck had eight of their eleven children. Our families had been camping in various parks in northern California. This particular day we had left our camping trailers in a Point Reyes Station campground and we were all driving out to Point Reyes Lighthouse. On the way we stopped at an oyster farm on Drakes Bay. The man behind the counter asked me if I wanted to purchase any oysters. I said, "We're camping and I have no way to cook them!"

He asked, "Do you have a grill?"

I said, "Yes."

"Ok", he said, "Place the <u>fresh</u> oysters opening side up on the grill over the charcoal. When the oyster opens up and steam comes out they're done and ready to eat with a little butter. The little ones that are <u>fresh</u> work the best."

In my most agreeable I'll try anything once voice, I said, "Give me a dozen, no wait! Give me two dozen." Then rapidly thinking about how many people we would have at supper, I said, "No make it three dozen!" As the man started to pick out five to eight inch long oysters, I said, "I thought you said the little ones worked the best?"

He responded, "Yes, the twelve inch long ones don't cook up as well over a grill."

Just then Chuck walked in and asked what I was doing?

"I'm buying three dozen fresh oysters!"

He said, "Give me three dozen too!"

As we walked out I began to ponder how we were going to eat seventy-two six inch long oysters, especially since we had already bought steaks for supper. I imagined we would have the smelliest trashcan in the campground.

That evening Chuck and I set our charcoal braziers next to one another with a bottle of scotch between us and we told the kids that everyone had to try at least one oyster before they could have their steak! The kids immediately fell in love with the oysters dipped in a little butter. By the end of the evening all of the oysters and steaks were gone. With kids and food you don't always get so lucky, but this time we had made a lucky decision.

CAMPING NEAR 29 PALMS

I was in one of those half dreaming states where you can't really control your movements or yell. My arms were flailing against the sides of the tube tent and I think I was groaning. I heard a crunching sound! At first I thought it might be an animal, until my dream saturated mind translated the rhythmic sound into footsteps. It sounded like someone was walking on a thin crust of frost or snow. The only trouble was it was about forty degrees Fahrenheit, and there was no snow crust on the ground. What was going on here?

All the kids were apparently sound asleep. The fire had probably died down to bright red embers with an occasional pop and crack as the logs collapsed under their own weight in the intense glowing heat. The sky was still pitch black. The cloud cover obscured the millennium of stars that I knew were overhead, so that in the glowing light of the embers one couldn't see much beyond the ends of the surrounding cluster of cheap tube tents.

Chuck and I had walked our kids about four miles into the desert for a weekend campout. It was probably after midnight, early Saturday morning.

It has always amazed me just how dark and totally black night can be without some stars or moonshine. We city folks just don't know what real darkness is until we get away from the glow of the city and out under a totally cloud covered sky which shuts out all of those trillions of little pinpoints of light.

Maybe small rodents were into some of our backpacks after food, and maybe what I took for footstep sounds were those mice running around. I sure didn't want to awaken the whole campsite for a couple of mice.

Something was obviously moving around out there, something was not right.

I've heard rodents in our food supply before in the High Sierras, and this really didn't sound like a small creature chewing through a package of freeze dried food.

The heavy hand of slumber was too powerful and it pulled me back under the shroud of sleep.

We had planned a long weekend trip to Joshua Tree National Monument campground, but all the campsites were taken. Our first alternative, if the campground was full, was to climb Mount San Jacinto and camp at 10,000 foot Round Valley; but threatening rain and snow didn't seem to be too compatible with tube tents at that altitude. Our third alternative had been just a simple walk out into the desert, camp overnight and return the next day, unless we found water, then we could stay a second night. To supplement our individual canteens, we bought a two and a half gallon plastic "Jerry" jug at a hardware store in Twenty Nine Palms. We also stopped at the local US Park Service Ranger Station to obtain suggestions for where we might begin our hike. The Ranger was most cooperative and directed us to an area that he felt was a fairly easy hike.

I had brought Dennis, Dan, Therese and Margaret. The kids all got along nicely and they were all at a good age for hiking and camping.

Chuck and family were not too familiar with backpacking, but a four mile walk into the desert, lugging a jug of water just requires a desire to get away from it all, not a whole lot of expertise. I had the compass and backpacking experience.

Each of us had a backpack with plenty of freeze dried food, warm clothing, tube tent and a sleeping bag. Our biggest problem, we thought at the time was the water. We parked Chuck's VW bus out of sight from the highway to minimize the chance of vandalism and then headed due east, sighting on a large hill about two miles distant and walking directly toward it. Occasionally we took rear sightings as we walked to make sure we had coordinates for our return trip to the bus.

Most backpacking is done in areas where water exists either from a stream or spring. It's amazing how heavy two and a half gallons of water can get when coupled with a thirty pound pack on your back.

Upon arriving at the hill we found a pass and on the other side sighted on another large hill three miles distant. In the early afternoon we arrived at a wash at the end of the large hill's alluvial fan and decided the soft sand would make a great place for a camp.

The afternoon had been spent exploring and then settling down for supper.

When the kids rose in the morning, two of the girls returned from their toilet and their giggling started to roust the others. Margaret yelled out, "Dad, which one of us has on cowboy boots?"

"What do you mean? None of us are wearing cowboy boots!" I answered.

"Dad, there are cowboy boot footprints circling all around our tent!"

I got up and walked over to her tent. There in the soft sand were cowboy boot footprints circling each of our seven tents. The cowboy footprints were imprinted on top of our footprints made the day before, as if someone had been searching for somebody. By this time Chuck was up and inspecting the footprints also. He quietly called me back to our campfire and asked, "Were you up at all last night?"

I answered, "No!"

He then asked, "Did you see anyone?"

"No, but I heard something." I responded. I couldn't contain himself any longer, "Look, I had the darnest nightmare last night. I dreamt that someone was walking around our campsite. It made me very upset and anxious, but I couldn't seem to bring myself out of my dream world state. I tried to yell out but couldn't. I even flung out my arms to chase whoever was out there away. I was real uncomfortable about who was walking around. I think I was afraid of being harmed or that harm might come to the kids. It seemed the footsteps were walking right next to my tent. The footsteps sounded like they were walking on frost or a thin crust of snow, a kind of crisp squishing sound. Now this morning I see all these footprints! What was going on out here last night?"

"I don't know," said Chuck.

"Do you want to stick around another night and stay up to see if he or it returns?" I half jokingly inquired.

Chuck didn't think I was funny.

I said, "We don't really have enough water to stay another day; and that dream I had really upset me. I was fearful of what was going on! I really don't know if we were in danger or not, but I don't want to go through another night like that. A night that I can't rationally explain. What I really don't understand is how my subconscious mind during my dream seemed to have been aware of a presence walking around right outside of my tent. This reality is kind of frightening. Lets get out of here before the kids hear us and they get frighten also."

A NEW YEARS EVE IN A CLOSET

Dianne and I went to a New Years Eve party leaving our oldest, Debbie, as the daughter in charge. Debbie was on restriction for some infraction over this mid 70's holiday; and thus available for sitting. All four of the younger children were downstairs in our TV room watching the evening celebrations, with permission to stay up to see the New Year come in. Shortly after Dianne and I left, Debbie excused herself stating she was tired and went to her room. Unbeknownst to the younger children she cleaned out her closet and in the place of clothes set up a small table and chairs in the closet lit by candles. At a prearranged time she let her boy friend Ron in the front door and secreted him upstairs into the closet. As the younger children watched TV, she and Ron celebrated with cola and candy in the closet. As they finished pieces of candy they flung the wrappers out onto the bedroom floor leaving a pile of evidence. At one point, Mary, the seconded oldest daughter, came upstairs to see what Debbie was doing. Seeing all the candy wrappers, Mary exclaimed, "I know what you are doing!" Meaning her sister was eating candy without sharing it with her or the other children.

Debbie thinking she had been found out pleaded with Mary not to disclose who was in the closet with her. Upon opening the closet door further, Mary discovers Ron, but agrees not to tell if she can get some of the candy.

The evening progresses with Mary making periodic trips upstairs for more candy while the younger children watch TV downstairs.

Right after midnight, Ron is secreted out the front door before the younger ones are sent upstairs and off to bed.

We found out about this incident years later after Debbie was married.

MY MICKEY MOUSE SOCKS

It was the day before my oldest daughter's wedding. Her bags were packed and she was about to take her things over to their apartment. All of a sudden I knew I had to get into her locked suitcase. While everyone was down stairs I went up to her bedroom and managed to unlock her suitcase. Sure enough, there they were, my Mickey Mouse socks. That brazen young bride to be was making a final statement of independence and one final attempt to steal my favorite pair of Mickey Mouse socks.

This battle had been going on since she was a teenager. I would wear my Mickey Mouse socks given to me as a birthday present, put them in the laundry and then they never seemed to make it back to my sock drawer. Our oldest folded socks as one of her weekly chores. Though I would make numerous inquiries, no one seemed to ever know anything about my MM socks. Then one day there they were in the dryer, I retrieved them, wore them once, put them in the laundry and they disappeared again. One day in a very suspicious mood I looked in my oldest daughter's sock drawer and there were my MM socks. Thereafter I always knew where to look. I had to be quick though, a couple times I stopped her going out the front door to catch the school bus and forced her to take off my MM socks.

She would say, "Dad, please, I'm late, I'll miss my bus!"

But I never showed any mercy, I would say, "I don't care if you miss the bus and have to walk to school, take off my Mickey Mouse socks!"

Today, twenty-one years later, though she still shows no remorse, I still have and own my well patched favorite pair of Mickey Mouse socks. (I now have to watch Dianne, for fear she'll throw away my well patched favorites.)

CAMPING AT ALBEE CREEK

It was a two family vacation adventure. We, towing our Nimrod tent trailer and Chuck's family towing a small utility trailer containing their two tents and personal belongings. Our first night was spent at Brandon Island State Park along the Sacramento River in the Sacramento Delta area. I didn't realize that Chuck's family was intent on setting up their two tents and starting their evening meal before the Millers got their Nimrod all unfolded. The first night Chuck's family won hands down. The Millers held their own on subsequent nights.

The second night we found campsites at Albee Creek State Park in the Northern California Redwoods. Albee Creek Park was on the site of a former homestead that had an meadow orchard of productive apple trees and numerous black berry vines alongside a flowing stream. Our tents were set up among the redwoods and pines. Each morning we walked over to the meadow and picked a bowl of ripe black berries to go on our Grapenuts flakes. Hikes through the redwoods were spectacular whether taken early in the morning mists or in the cool evening shadows. We were all very fortunate on this camping trip for there were a minimum of flying critters during our short stay. After a fun day of hiking or exploring we would go down to the orchard after supper and pick a spot to watch the does and fawns come out from the woods and eat the fallen apples. As long as we were quiet the deer would feed on the apples. If a fawn got too close to a human, mother doe would come over and nudge her fawn away from the dangerous human being. The bucks seldom showed themselves, and if they did they stayed very close to the edge of the woods and cover.

Chuck's family tried to go back on subsequent summers and capture again the magic of Albee Creek, but either the apples were wormy, or the berries had ripened early that year, or the flying critters drove them crazy day and night.

We were lucky that summer. We captured the magic of Albee Creek on our first visit.

THE DOG IS IN THE HOUSE

It was after midnight and Dianne told me Queenie, our very large all white German Shepherd, was in the house. I responded, "Impossible! I locked all the doors myself." I got up and sure enough there was the dog at the bottom of the stairs. I went down and looked at both doors to the back yard. They both appeared locked. Then I looked into the downstairs bedroom where sixteen-year-old Dennis appeared to be in bed asleep. How in the world did the dog get into the locked house? Then I actually pulled on each outside door and the downstairs bathroom door was not latched. Suspicious, I carefully checked my son Dennis and sure enough pillows were under the blankets. I immediately went out the unlatched door and there was my eldest son quietly pushing our station wagon backwards down the street before he started it. By the time I got upstairs, dressed and went out the front door he was gone. I stood on the driveway and asked myself, if I was a sixteen year old again at 12:45 AM, where would I go? In a flash I thought, Of course! I got into the other car and drove to our nearest hamburger stand. And there swaggering up to the inside counter was the hungry sixteen year old King of the Road. I sat there looking at him and tried to think of what I should do. I could go home and go back to bed and talk to him in the morning-or I could drive up and embarrass him before the young lady working the night shift-or I could park my car and steal my station wagon back and let him walk home. I chose the latter. As I was slowly driving the wagon out of the parking lot the girl at the counter told him someone was stealing his car. He came charging out and stopped dead when he saw who was behind the wheel. I waved him over and asked for the key. Then I asked where he had obtained the key and he said he had duplicated it one day when he was running errands. I then asked for his driver's license and told him he was on restriction. After I got him home I had to wake Dianne to help me retrieve the other car still parked near the hamburger stand. In as much as he never took a vehicle again without permission, I guess it was a reasonable solution.

MY OLDEST SON, THE MECHANIC

Dennis was a junior in high school in 1974, when he bought his first car. He asked me if I would buy him a car. I said, "No". Dennis had been riding my 1965 Honda trial bike, and it just didn't take the place of a car.

He said, "Mike's father is going to buy him one!"

I said, "That's OK, but I'm not buying you one. If you want a car, then save your money and buy it yourself. And don't forget you will also have to buy the car insurance."

George, a friend of the family had a 1962 Rambler straight six convertible that needed bodywork. One Sunday after Mass, he said he'd sell it to Dennis for $65.00. George had just put a new battery in the car, and when we went to pick up the car, he wanted to keep the new battery and put it in one of his other cars. But the battery terminals were in the wrong place so he had to leave the new battery in the Rambler. George told Dennis, "You are now buying a $30.00 car with a new $35.00 battery."

At this point in his life, Dennis just wanted wheels! He made no serious attempt to fix up the car body or put it in better running order. He did buy a convertible top from Sears so he could drive the car in rainy weather. When the brakes wore down low he made no attempt to get them fixed. In a short time the car became a safety hazard. In those days California still had sufficient funds to conduct spot Highway Patrol safety checkpoints. Dennis avoided these check points with a passion, for he knew if he got stopped his car would never pass.

One day I came home from work just as he had successfully adjusted the carburetor. He said, "You know Dad, I think I can fix just about anything I want to on this car."

I remember thinking, one adjusted carburetor does not a mechanic make.

Shortly thereafter, I came home one evening and his car had a blown head gasket. He wanted me to help him right then and there to take the head off and to put on a new head gasket. I told him I would help him on the weekend, because it was too big a job to do that evening. When I came home the next evening he had the engine head off and wanted me to help him put the new head gasket on right now! I told him we would have to get the flat head checked to make sure it was truly flat and not warped. I told him a warped head was probably the reason the head gasket blew in the first place. He wouldn't wait and when I got home the next night he had the engine all put back together, but it wouldn't start!

He said, "Dad, I know I put that engine back together perfectly, so why won't it start?"

I answered, "If it's put together correctly, it should start, and if it won't start it's not put together correctly."

He said, "I know I put it together just exactly right, I didn't make any mistakes!"

I didn't know what was wrong, but I again said, "Wait until Saturday and I'll help you figure out what's wrong."

On Saturday, we tore the engine down, and about half of the push rods were incorrectly placed and the valves weren't opening properly. I showed him how to correctly position the push rods, but again cautioned him to get the head checked for warpage before he put it back together. He wanted to use the car that Saturday night and insisted upon putting the head back on the way It was. Needless to say, within a week, he blew the head gasket again. This is the way it went for the next two years, Dennis only doing the bear bones minimum to keep the car running. The emergency brake was not hooked up, but just dangling under the dash board, the brake lights didn't work, turn signals didn't work, the windshield wipers didn't work, the brakes were very low and needed adjustment, the headlights didn't all work, etc...

One day in the spring of his senior year when he was working at a local Taco Bell, friend Mike asked to borrow his car to run home for a moment. Dennis gave him the keys and as you might expect Mike drove right into a CHP checkpoint. When Mike returned the keys, he also gave Dennis the CHP safety check form with almost all of the boxes checked indicating all of the repairs that were required. Someone told Dennis the CHP didn't follow-up on those safety checks and he shouldn't worry. I told Dennis, that a safety check with the number of violations indicated on his form would most certainly be followed up! I told him he would get about three follow up inquiries from the CHP asking him to bring the car to a CHP Station so they could verify that all of the repairs had been properly made. If he failed to respond, then a marshal would be at the front door one morning with a court summons to appear before a judge to explain why he had not complied with CHP's safety requests. I told him at that point he had better have a bunch of receipts indicating the repairs had all been done, and a good explanation for the judge as to why he had procrastinated so long in getting the repairs accomplished-or he better have a receipt from a junk yard indicating the car was junked and off the streets. And if he junked it, he should get to the court clerk before his summons date and show the court clerk the junkyard receipt and get himself removed from the court calendar. I said, "The last thing you want to do is to appear before that judge without a reasonable explanation as to why you have procrastinated so long!" One morning in May 1975, a marshal was at the front door with a court summons. Dennis immediately junked the car and showed the receipt to the court clerk and got himself removed from the court calendar.

I was relieved. I didn't know just how he had been driving when away from home, but one experience left a lot of questions in my mind. As I was coming home one evening down Los Flores approaching Stamey, just before I got to the intersection, a red Rambler convertible was coming so fast south bound on Stamey that it skidded broadside through the intersection and almost hit me head on. The driver was wide eyed as he realized he had just about crashed into his father!

Needless to say the junking of that red 1962 Rambler made driving in Southern California much safer than it had been for the previous two years.

OUR RUNAWAY SON

One summer morning near the end of his senior year, I asked eighteen-year-old Dennis to finish cleaning three window screens before he left for the beach. He complained that he was tired of being the family slave. An argument ensued and he declared he was leaving home. It was two weeks before his high school graduation and five weeks before he was to go into the Air Force which he had decided to join--to be free! He placed his belongings in brown paper bags stating we should notice that he was only taking old clothes because he wouldn't be going to church. He left, but in an hour he returned to use the phone. He stated he had no money and he wanted to call his Grandma Miller where he intended to stay until it was time to go into the Air Force.

Grandma wasn't home so he left again. I called the local YMCA and obtained their current board and room rates. When he returned the second time, to again call his grandmother, I suggested he could pay sixty dollars a week room and board, and he would not have to do any chores. Or, he could continue to live here for nothing as a participating member of the family. He indicated he had no money to pay room and board and he left again. He returned an hour later stating he couldn't get hold of Grandma. He reluctantly indicated he had no choice but to live at home for the next five weeks as a participating member of the family. I said, "Fine! Now as a participating member of the family, would you please go out and wash those three screens and then hang them back up on the windows."

He said, "Oh good grief." He went out, washed the screens and ten minutes later went off with his friends to the beach.

TEN SHILLINGS

The usher said, "Ten Shillings," and pointed toward a ticket booth at the end of the lobby.

We were spending our last night in Vienna. It was 1975 and Dianne and I were on a three-week Holy Year tour of Europe.

Ten Austrian shillings, or about 80 cents, didn't seem too bad a price to pay for what we thought was a look around the lobby of the world famous Vienna opera house.

On our way into Vienna (Wien in German) the day before, our Romantic Europe and Alpine Highlights tour guide had discouraged any of us from trying to get tickets to the Vienna opera. She said people wait as long as three months for tickets and that they are always sold out weeks ahead of time. Earlier the previous day in passing we had tried to get in to look at the interior of the building just so we could say we had seen the Vienna opera, but it was locked up tight.

A night at the Vienna opera was one of Dianne's must see on this tour. In retrospect, I guess we should have realized some reservations would be necessary, but in our usual naive optimism we had hoped to take what ever seats were available.

Dianne, I and another couple had decided to spend our last night in Vienna at a downtown park restaurant listening to Straus waltzes.

As the four of us were walking towards the park we passed the opera house, which was all lit up, but apparently, empty. Dianne wondered if the ushers would let us in to just look around. I reminded her of what the our tour director had said, that the place was sold out for months in advance, and that I doubted if they would allow us to wander around the lobby.

Dianne said, "All they can say is no," and proceeded to go through the door and across the lobby toward the usher standing at the bottom of the grand staircase. As she approached the German speaking Austrian usher to get permission to look around the lobby I figured I had better get in there and support her as best I could. Before I could get halfway across the lobby, she turns and comes toward me saying we can look around the lobby for ten shillings. She asked me how much that is and can we afford it? I make a quick calculation and say it's only about 80 cents a piece. So we walk up to the lobby ticket booth and I say, "10 Shillings," and hold up four fingers. The man looks at me blankly for a moment and reaches into a folder and brings out a book from which he tears out four receipts.

We paid our 40 Shillings and began to look around the ground floor lobby. Another usher comes up, looks at our four receipts and points up the stairs, saying, "Up."

I figure this is all the time we get on the first level, and we go up to the second level lobby. Another usher comes up and attempts to sell us two booklets in English, but I resist not sure why we need a program for a walking tour of the lobby. The second floor lobby is quite large and has a display of jewels which we proceed of look over until another usher comes over, looks at our tickets, points to the stairs and says, "Up."

"Well I figure this is the oddest building tour I've ever been on, but up we go up to the third level where another usher looks at our receipts and says, "Up!"

When we get to the fourth level, the usher looks at the receipts and says, "Up."

We didn't even bother stopping at the fifth level and went all the way to the top. As we are moving towards the top level, I hear singing and music, and wonder if a show is going on. The top level is a snack bar, and an usher looks at our tickets and says, "Down vun!"

Boy! What a nutty place! So back down we go to the last level where an usher looks at our tickets, puts a finger over his lips to signal silence, and beckons us to follow him. He takes us into the side of a upper most gallery and leaves us standing behind red velvet railings looking down on the entire opera house and the stage and performance far below. I now realize we have purchased, not a simple tour of the lobbies, but standing room gallery positions. We were all delighted. Dianne is beaming from ear to ear!

As our eyes grew accustomed to the darkness we see some spaces off to our right in the center and we move over there. We began to realize we are in the student gallery at the very top most part of the opera house. At the intermission, the students and occupants leave handkerchiefs, scarves and other markers to show that space has been taken. Looking down we can see the first floor occupants in their formal evening gowns and tuxedos. The formal dress carried right up to the upper most gallery. At least 40% of the upper most gallery seats were in formal attire.

The four of us moved around to the right side where it appeared no one had claimed space and settled down to wait for the start of the second half of the program. The orchestra filed back in, the main floor and various gallery levels again filled up with their formal attired occupants and the program resumed with *Palachi.*

I have never been much of an opera fan, but half-way through the second part of the program, the precision of the orchestra and the singing made a opera convert out of me.

I felt, I could actually begin to like this stuff.

A CHILD'S DIRECTIONS

In the late Spring of 1975 Holy Year, Dianne and I had left our three week tour of Europe in Rome and were trying to find a convent school on the west side of Rome. Being short of cash, we took a trolley to the general vicinity of the school and then proceeded the rest of the way on foot carrying our luggage. As we walked the narrow streets our English inquiries to a policeman and later to a mailman brought only impatient replies in Italian, which we didn't understand, with vague hand signals pointing us in the general direction of our destination. After a while, in frustration, we stopped a girl of ten and showed her the slip of paper with the address. Her response was immediate and delightful. With a child's uninhibited enthusiasm and a big smile she indicated the street we must follow using two fingers to indicate us walking. Then she formed an arch with her arms and showed us we must pass under it. She then indicated us making a right turn and following that street until we came to a flight of stairs. She motioned with her fingers how we must walk up the flight and then turn right at the top and follow the road down the hill to the school. I repeated the directions in hand signals back to her to show we understood. Fifteen minutes later we were at our destination, just in time to catch a special bus to the first meeting of our religious conference.

A child's big smile and totally uninhibited hand signals were much better than a detailed street map, and much more enjoyable.

A SHORT RIDE ON THE ORIENT EXPRESS

On a Friday in May 1975, Dianne and I had left our three-week tour of Europe to attend a three day Charismatic Conference at an area outside of Rome near the Saint Callosities catacombs. The conference ended late on Sunday and we had planned to leave Rome at 6:00 PM on Monday by train to Milan and then on to Brig, Switzerland where we were to arrive at 2:38 AM. At 8:00 AM Tuesday morning we were to meet our bus driver at the Hotel Victoria. The bus was scheduled to pick up the guide and the tour group at the Visp, Switzerland train station at 9:00 AM, as they returned from an overnight stay in Zermatt.

The train left Rome at 6:30 PM a half an hour late. I was concerned because we had a tight forty-five minute train change to make in Milan. The train we were on was scheduled to stop in the Lambratti Station in Milan, and our train to Brig was to depart from the Garibaldi Station (or so our Travel Agent in Whittier had mistakenly told us). We thought we had to take a cab to the Garibaldi Station and losing a half hour of our precious forty-five minute connection time at the onset of the trip worried me. If we did not make the connection in Milan, there was no train stopping in Brig until 9:00 AM Tuesday morning and we would have missed our bus. We would then have had to go on our own by train to Lucerne where we could meet up with the tour group late Wednesday. We were running short on money, and I was very apprehensive about traveling on our own in a country where I didn't speak the language.

In the Rome train station we met two priests from Windsor, Ontario, Canada. We had recognized them as having been at the conference. While on the train, Dianne and I joined them in their compartment for a snack. The train kept stopping and eventually an announcement was made in Italian that the train would be an hour late getting into Milan. Of course we did not understand the announcement at that point in time. We had related to the priests about our train connections and an Italian lady who was in the same compartment overheard our conversation and told us about the train's delayed arrival. She volunteered to speak to the train conductor on our behalf. The conductor informed us via the lady that our train for Brig stopped in the Central Station, not the Garibaldi Station, and if we had gone as planned to the Garibaldi Station we would have missed the train anyway! He then said the train we were on passed through the Central Station on the way to its scheduled stop in the Lambratti Station. He also related that the train we wished to catch to Brig originated in Istanbul and it was most always late. If it had not yet arrived or if it were still in the Central Station as we passed through, he would ask the engineer to make an unscheduled stop so we could jump off. He wouldn't know for sure what he could do for us until we got into the Milan Central Station. Needless to say we were on pins and needles for the rest of the trip. Where else but in Italy would a conductor offer to make an unscheduled stop for two Americans.

Just before we left home we had seen the movie, *Murder on the Orient Express*! And now here we were trying to make connection with that train that ran from Istanbul to Paris and which had been so famous for so many years. I had heard that the train and it's service had degraded in recent years, but still it was exciting!

As our train slowed coming into the Central Station, the conductor came back and asked us to follow him up forward toward the engine where he could quickly communicate with the engineers. The Italian lady came along to translate and the two priests said they would come along and pray! As the train came into the Central Station, the crew realized the Orient Express (as I decided to call it) was still sitting in the station and braked hard to a stop! The conductor told us to jump off and I said, "Jump off and go where?" The conductor said as translated by the lady, "Go down the stairs into the subway, turn left, go over two tracks and back up, and hurry!" As we were running down the subway a Milan stationmaster was running toward the engine yelling something in Italian which I surmised to be an admonishment about the train making an unscheduled stop. We had fortunately lightened our luggage for our short three-day stay in Rome to one suitcase. I put this on my head and we both ran down into the subway, over two tracks and up onto a darken platform. The train on the left was dark and dead looking, while the one on the right, while also dark, had a train conductor swinging a lantern about two cars up.

I yelled, "Wait," and we both ran to the last open door. I said, "Brig, Switzerland?" and the conductor looked at me in a non-comprehending manner. I showed him my tickets and said, "Brig in die Swisse", he indicated we should get aboard. He said, "Primo class", and indicated that we should follow him forward. As we walked through the non air conditioned cars it was hot and sultry, beer bottles were rolling around the corridors, babies were crying and I wasn't too impressed with this famous train. Dianne asked me if we were on the right train? I said I didn't know! As the conductor showed us to our compartment I asked him what time we arrived in Brig, and he indicated he didn't understand English and left. I still wasn't sure if we were going back south toward Rome or north toward Switzerland. It was now 12:45 AM and my wife said she was going to pray and trust in the Lord and shortly thereafter fell asleep. I got a map out and looked up the name of some towns that we would pass through if we were on the right train. One of the first major stops would be Stressa, Italy on Lake Maggiore. In about an hour we stopped in Stressa. North of Stressa the route split, and if the train's next stop was Domodossola, we were on the right train and headed toward Brig. As the train stopped in what I hoped was Domodossola I could not see the station sign so I walked aft a couple cars so I could see the name of the station, and there it was, Domodossola! We were on the right train! When we left Domodossola, a very big Italian policeman asked to see our passports, but spoke no English. About five minutes later, two very big Swiss policemen in plainclothes asked to see our passports, and appeared to be looking for someone. I thought, *Wow! detectives on the Orient Express looking for someone, maybe it hasn't lost all of it's glamour!* It was over an hour and a half since we had gotten on this train and only now did I begin to relax a little.

We arrived in Brig abruptly at 2:38 AM and we hurried to get off. The Brig stop was scheduled for two minutes, and in exactly two minutes the train began to move again. We walked across the street to the Hotel Victoria. The front lobby door was locked. I rang and rang the night bell and finally a porter answered and let us in. A piece of paper with my name on it was on the front desk with a key beside it. I said, "Miller, that's me", grabbed the key, declining to sign in saying I would do it in the morning, and we went up to our room. We got a shower and a wonderful four hours of sleep, and met our bus driver the next morning for our ride to Visp to meet the rest of the tour group.

If we hadn't spoken to two priests on the train platform in Rome, and if we hadn't had a sandwich with them in their compartment, and if an English speaking Italian lady hadn't spoken to the conductor on our behalf, and if the Orient Express hadn't been an hour late that night, and if an Italian conductor and engineer hadn't taken pity on two Americans and made an unscheduled 30 second stop in the Milan Central Station, and if in less than a minute we had not ran to the right train-we wouldn't have been sitting calmly in our tour bus on a lovely Tuesday morning in May 1975 on our way to Mount Pilatus, Switzerland. I just knew someone up there was really looking after us! Prayers really are answered!

LEAVING FOR THE AIR FORCE

During most of his high school years, oldest son Dennis would rush out of the house each morning with his socks and shoes in his hand. A completely dressed son in the morning leaving for school was not a common sight.

Dennis insisted in the latter part of his senior year upon joining the Air Force-to be free! He wanted freedom from parental control, especially freedom from household chores and rules-freedom He thought only the Air Force could provide.

We tried to convince him that he should give himself a little time to get out on his own after high school. His mother and I suggested he get a job-and if he wanted to leave home, then get an apartment, and experience what it is like to be free and to support himself. After a few months, if he still wanted to join the Air Force, to do so, with our blessings. But no, he wanted to commit himself in February of his senior year to leave for service training three weeks after high school graduation. He said this early commitment was necessary for him to get the electronic schooling he desired. Nothing could dissuade him. I finally reluctantly agreed to allow him to commit himself by signing my consent.

This way to freedom started out with a rough beginning. The day before Dennis understood he was suppose to report to the recruiting office in Whittier, he received a call from the recruiting sergeant asking him, "Where are you?" It seems he got the dates confused. He was supposed to report a day earlier than he thought. He was told to report the next morning.

The following morning he ran out of the house with shoes and socks in his hands as I rushed him to the recruiting office. As usual, he arrived late.

Later in the morning the recruiting sergeant called me at work and informed me Dennis had forgotten his birth certificate and other papers which he had to have immediately in the central recruiting office in Los Angeles. I explained that no one was at home that day. The sergeant then asked me to go home and get the papers and drive the documents into Los Angeles. I explained I had work that I couldn't leave for that long. I offered to meet him at our house and give him the papers. I told the sergeant he would have to get the papers to Dennis. He unhappily answered that he guessed Dennis was now his problem-I agreed. When the sergeant got to LA, Dennis's bus had already left for the airport. He finally caught up with him at LAX.

In the evening when I told Dianne what happen, we smilingly agreed, he was now the Air Force's problem-to get him up and moving in the morning.

WHAT DID YOU DO WITH MY GIRL SCOUT MESS KIT?

My youngest daughter, Marque, would say so convincingly, "Dad, what did you do with my Girl Scout mess kit?"

My response would be to immediately ask her if she looked in her closet? Her response was always, "Yes, it's not there-I remember distinctly giving it to you to put it away the last time I went camping with the Girl Scouts-so it wouldn't get lost."

She always sounded so sure of herself and so convincing that I would believe her and try to remember where I might have put it. I would search the house attic, then the garage overhead where some camping equipment was stored. After spending at least a half an hour and exhausting every place I could think of to look, I would say, "Marque, I've looked everywhere, I can't find it. Are you sure you really gave it to me? Did you really look good in your room?"

Her answer was always so positive and convincing, "Yes Dad, I looked all over my room real good, it's not there!"

I would walk in her room, look in her closet, lift one garment off a hook and there was the mess kit.

Now the sad part of this whole scenario is it happened more than once. It was always months between Girl Scout campouts and I would fall for her convincing statements every time. By the time I finally wised up to her, she was through with Girl Scout campouts.

TEENAGE LOGIC

As I examined our damaged station wagon, I lamented over the questionable value of a vehicle of this type that now had a rear tail gate hatch that would no longer fully open. I was becoming increasingly irritated over the extent of the damage.

Therese, who had been driving the wagon, attempted to calm me with the logic, "Dad, I don't see why you are getting so upset, I carefully looked at the post I backed into, and I could see by the scratches that a lot of other people had backed into that same post before me!"

INTRIGUE AT THE TEL AVIV AIRPORT

It was June 1979, and we were returning home from Israel with our tour group via British Airways by way of a one-night stop in London. As tour leaders we had spent the last three weeks leading a group of 72 through Israel, and Mount Sinai. The group was tired and we were all ready to go home. In the Tel Aviv Airport security was intense. Dianne, Margaret and I, as a family, were separately screened by a security person in a private booth before we were allowed to progress into the departing portion of the terminal. If a person leaves or steps away from their bags for only a moment, the bag is immediately picked up by security personnel. If the owner cannot be readily identified the bag is removed from the terminal.

The airplanes are randomly spotted around the airport tarmac which is suppose to make it more difficult for terrorists to know which planes are going to which destinations. When the flight is ready to depart all passengers are loaded onto trams and driven out to the plane by a circuitous route. As we were descending a stairs to board our tram I stumbled over a military style duffel bag which had been abandoned on the stairs. By the time I was at the bottom of the stairs, the abandoned bag had already been confiscated by airport security. Why would anyone bring a carry on bag all the way through security and just before they are to get on a tram to go to their aircraft, they abandon the bag on a stairway. Very very suspicious! We boarded the plane and the three of us were seated just aft of the wing on the right side. As the full plane sat on the tarmac on this very hot morning, the fuel began to boil out of overflow vents on the top of the wing. Then I heard the baggage compartment below us being reopened and the handlers were taking all the baggage out of the plane and spreading it out on the tarmac. We continued to wait, and soon so much fuel was boiling out of the wings that the handlers had to move the baggage away from the large puddle of fuel that was forming below the wing. I thought this posed a very real fire danger. Then two security cars drove up and the security personnel with a young lady walked up and down the rows of baggage in a manner that suggested she was being made to pick out her bags. Once her bags were retrieved, her bags and she were driven off. The baggage was reloaded onto the airplane and we took off for London. The flight took about five hours and Dianne, Margaret and I moved around and changed places numerous times. Seated behind us next to the window, with two vacant seats to her left and apparently traveling alone, was a young lady who hardly moved from her seat during the entire flight.

At one point, the Captain, a bearded Scotsman, came back and visited with the passengers. When he came up to us I asked him what had gone on back on the tarmac and the off-loading of the baggage. He said that the Airport Security and the Israeli equivalent of our FBI had asked that the baggage belonging to a young lady they were detaining be off-loaded. He said that all the baggage had to be taken off the plane to find her bags. As soon as the Captain left, the girl sitting behind me leaned forward and asked me what the Captain had said about the girl on the tarmac. I told her what the Captain had said and she sat back and stayed in her seat for the remainder of the flight. Upon arriving in London, it was a long walk from the plane to the passport control booths. As the three of us were walking along I noticed that the young girl that had sat behind us was walking with a man that she appeared to know. I thought that was strange, for if she knew someone on the long flight, why had she remained by herself all during the entire flight when there were two seats right next to her that were vacant. As we approached the passport control booths, the line bunched-up a bit and I heard the man behind me tell her, "Once we are past here (the passport booths), we are home free". I immediately became very suspicious, for the young lady behind me had been very curious about what the Captain had said about the girl on the tarmac-she sat alone on a long flight even though she apparently knew someone on the plane very well-and now she and her male companion were worried about getting pass a passport control booth. I quickly asked myself, should I get involved? Should I tell the passport control booth personnel about my observations and suspicions? If I did take the time to explain what I had observed and heard, it would stop and back up the line and in the end would I look foolish? Further, I had a tour group to take home and I would have a problem if I found myself detained in London because of what I might be becoming involved with. I also had to make contact with a bus driver at the terminal entrance to get our two-bus tour group of 72 people to the hotel on Baker Street in London. As I came up to the passport control I said nothing and the pair behind me were subsequently passed through. I have often wondered what that pair and the girl on the Tel Aviv tarmac were involved in? Would my becoming involved have prevented some smuggling or terrorist act? Which one of them abandoned the duffel bag on the stairs-why was it abandoned and what was in it? I will never know!

CHAPTER 9
My Fifties
(The 1980's)

A POINT LOMA PRAYER MEETING

Our family attended a weekend healing and prayer meeting type of retreat at Point Loma near San Diego, California, led by Father Francis McNutt and Agnes Sanford. One evening we attended a healing session wherein a number of teams were chosen to pray for various people asking for prayer. Dianne and I were asked to pray for a young girl who had been badly scarred from burns received during an automobile accident. As we were praying, Dianne motioned me to move my hand over her heart. As I did so, I felt a silver dollar size warmth in the center of my palm. When I moved my hand away from her heart the sensation of warmth on my palm left. When I moved my hand back over her heart, the sensation of warmth about two inches in diameter returned. We both felt this warmth and believed it was a sign that healing was occurring. This was the first and only time I have ever felt warmth such as this during a healing session.

A SQUEAL OF DELIGHT

It was 1980, we were on our second trip to Israel, and Dianne and I had just finished an afternoon of shopping in the Jewish section of Jerusalem just west of the old city. We had a number of packages, no taxi was in sight, so we decided to walk and look for a cab. Our hotel was the Intercontinental on the Mount of Olives, just east of the old city across the Kiddron Valley. When we got to the Jaffa Gate of the old city, we still had not seen a cab. I suggested we walk through the old city and try to find a cab at an east gate. We had walked almost all the way through and were approaching the Saint Stephen gate just north of the temple mount when a little Arab girl held out her hand. It appeared that her mother was standing next to a building and allowing her cute little three or four year old to beg! I had accumulated a large number of Israeli coins in my left pocket which probably weren't worth much more than a couple dollars. Both hands were full, so I quickly shuffled packages to free my left hand, plunged it in my pocket without breaking my stride and grabbed as many coins as I could in one motion. While pulling my fist full of coins out of my pocket a number fell on the ground as I deposited the coins into this little girl's outstretched and cupped hands. To this day I can still remember the squeal of delight as what appeared to her to be a massive treasure was placed into her hands. She immediately ran to her mother joyfully displaying what she had just received. Her mother hurried into the narrow street to pick up the coins that I and the little girl had dropped. Although I had not given her that much money that joyful squeal of delight will always remain with me.

MOVIE OR PARTY?

One Friday evening my youngest daughter asked to use our Station Wagon to go to a movie with the girl across the street. I agreed, stating she was to be home by eleven. When I got into the wagon the next morning I noticed a crumpled wad of paper on the passenger side floor and keeping a tidy car I picked it up to throw it in the waste paper bag. Becoming curious, I unfolded it to examine the paper. It was a map to a party the night before. I walked back into the house and asked my daughter how she liked the movie. She said it was great. I said, "What did you think of the bearded psychologist?" She answered stating he was interesting. I said, "There was no bearded psychologist in that movie. Now I want the truth about the party!" She immediately confessed and wanted to know how I had found out and if her girlfriend's parents had told me. I said, "No they had not, but you just remember young lady, we parents have ways of finding things out and we know what's going on!" It was long after she was married with kids of her own, before I finally admitted I had found the discarded party map on the floor of the car and guessed she and her girl friend had gone to a party and not to a movie.

AMAZING BUT BORING

One of our last long distance trips in our 1973 Impala Station Wagon was towing the Nimrod tent trailer to Grand Island and back. Only Marque and Danny were with us on that trip. On the way we visited Boulder Dam, the Grand Canyon, and Durango and rode its steam locomotive to Silverton, a visit to Colorado Springs, etc... Our two teenagers stretched out in the back offered a singular bored continual commentary on all the wonderful sights along the way. To Dianne's pointing out of a beautiful and colorful sight would be the drifting forward comment from the back of the wagon, "Amazing, but boring." To almost every wonder pointed out-from Arizona's Painted Desert to the deepest part of the Grand Canyon, nothing escaped the label, "Amazing, but boring." To their teenage level of interest everything on that trip got the same disinterested evaluation.

TRUST YOUR BOY SCOUT

It was July 1982, and Dianne and I were leading our last tour through the Greek Aegean Isles. We were on Mykonos, a beautiful mountainous island whose main port had a wonderful white washed town whose extremely narrow streets were an absolute maze. Supposedly the town was laid out in a maze to confuse raiding pirates who were reluctant to venture very far into the twisting narrow streets, some only six feet wide, for fear of getting lost and thus captured. Dianne and I were attempting to cross this town to get some pictures of the world famous Mykonos windmills on its south eastern flank. As we walked through the streets, Dianne wanted to ask directions for she felt we were getting lost. But I kept telling her I didn't need directions and to trust her Boy Scout, as we twisted our way across town. She was convinced we were lost and continued chiding me to stop and ask directions. I kept saying, "Trust your Boy Scout." After about twenty minutes we came to a narrow street leading up hill and Dianne didn't want to bother walking up the hill unless she had to. I walked up the hill while she waited at the bottom, and upon reaching the top waved her to come up. There in front of me were the famous windmills. She was amazed that I found my way through the unfamiliar maze of streets that were known to confuse even the ancient pirates. Then I confessed. As we were walking through the narrow streets and alleys I was watching the sun's shadow on the buildings above me. It was late enough in the day I that I could tell which direction was west by the sun's shadow, and with that bit of information I simply followed a curving south easterly course through the village until we arrived at its south eastern end and the windmills.

A CONTAGIOUS ACT

Daughter Debbie was in the habit of bringing granddaughter Cynthia and grandson Gregory for a visit every Monday evening. Six year old Cynthia would voluntarily lie down on the sofa between 7:30

and 8:00 PM and go to sleep. Whereas four year old little Gregory would first fight sleep for a while and then eventually go to sleep on his blanket where ever he was at. One evening he was yawning, acting fussy and fighting the Sandman. I deliberately yawned loudly, Debbie immediately picked up on what I was doing and she also yawned. Then, wife Dianne became aware of what we were doing and she too yawned. I again yawned and Gregory yawned. By the time Debbie and Dianne yawned a second time, Gregory had laid his head on his blanket and was fast asleep. During a visit a week later the granddaughter again went to sleep on her own, while Gregory was again fighting the sleep process. I once more started the yawning, Debbie yawned, then Dianne. Gregory stopped playing, looked at each of us and said, "Stop that!"

THE FIREMAN

Oldest son Dennis obtained a firefighter position in the small Midwest town of Grand Island, Nebraska which has three fire stations. Periodically the fire department would stage demonstrations of their fire fighting techniques for family members and the public. Dennis invited his wife, two daughters and three year old son Adam to the show. As the most junior member of his station, it was his job to start the fire in the training tower, then the engine rolled up and the firemen put out the fire. The demonstration went very well and all were impressed. Days later my grandson was asked what his father did and he replied, "My daddy's a fireman, he lights the fires". It took months to reorient this young man about his father's job, for he was convinced that whenever the fire engine rolled, his father had set the fire.

THE IMPORTANCE OF A MASSAGE

When I was a child my mother would massage my back to help me get to sleep. Naturally I grew up liking and enjoying a back massage. I met and married a young lady who also enjoyed having her back and feet massaged. When Dianne wished to calm one of our six infants, she would lay the baby on her lap and slowly rub their backs. Of course these six children grew up liking their backs massaged.

Unfortunately, not all of our sons and daughters married partners that shared the same need for this type of physical relaxation. The importance again came to our attention recently when oldest daughter Debbie asked us to sit six year old grandson Gregory and eight year old granddaughter, Cynthia. Debbie wanted them in bed with lights out by 8:30 P.M. She said all we had to do was to promise to rub their feet for two minutes and they would be asleep in less than a minute. When the appointed time arrived and as I prepared to start rubbing my granddaughter's feet she asked me to make a promise. If she fell asleep before the two minutes were up, she wanted me to keep rubbing even though she was asleep so that she would get her full two minutes of foot massage. I started rubbing granddaughter Cynthia's feet and she was asleep in thirty seconds, and Dianne had grandson Gregory asleep within forty-five seconds. We gave an extra grandparent measure and rubbed both of their feet for another five minutes.

KEYS LOCKED IN MY DAUGHTER'S CAR

One evening around midnight my youngest daughter called from work lamenting that she had locked her keys in her car. She wanted me to drive her to a restaurant where her roommate worked to borrow her apartment key, then to their apartment where she had an extra set of car keys, than back to the restaurant to return her roommates key. And finally back to her employer's parking lot to retrieve her car. After an hour and a half of driving we arrived back at her car, whereupon she had a recollection she wasn't sure she wanted to tell me about at that moment. With reassurances that I wouldn't get upset, she confessed she just remembered she had hidden a spare car key in a magnetic box under the front bumper. She had hidden it there so long ago she had forgotten all about it. I guess this is why fathers get grayer when called because they respond so easily and don't get upset.

CHAPTER 10
My Sixties
(The 1990's)

A DREAM ABOUT MY MOM

Shortly after my Mom's death in March 1991, I had a dream. As I exited the bathroom of her house, she was standing in the hallway just outside the door looking at me. Shocked, I shouted at her, "You don't belong here any more!" Meaning you're dead, you don't belong here.

I've often wondered what the dream would have been like if I hadn't rejected her presence so violently. Did I drive her spirit out of her house?

MOM'S HAUS

As I stood in the front room, I drank in my feelings about this fifty year old house. It came to me that this home had seen lots of love. Lots of living had happened here! A lot of my relatives lived between these walls. My father died while living here-the last occupying person being my mother. .

It was early fall of 1991, my mother had died on March 31st. We, the heirs, had decided not to fix the house up, but to sell it as is. David's kids preferred to have the money right now, and I and LeRoy weren't too excited about all the painting and work it would take to put it in 100% right order. So we sold it at a good price, as later market factors would show.

If a house could absorb love in its walls, then this house was filled to over flowing with love. I wondered if the new owners would be able to feel it as I felt it at this moment. I felt good about my mother and the life she had led in this house. She lived a good life, and lived here for all but the last thirty days which she spent in a convalescent hospital in La Habra. I knew when I walked out the front door it would be the last time I would be here-so I just stood there a few minutes and drank in the good feeling.

THE LOCKED APARTMENT SCREEN DOOR OR TWICE IN 41 YEARS

Shortly after we were married we lived in a small one-bedroom apartment in Long Beach, California. I was working a swing shift at an aerospace plant and I got home about 1:30 AM. On hot summer evenings, my young wife would open the backdoor to the apartment, hook its screen door from the inside, thus allow more air to circulate through the apartment and provide some additional cooling. When she went to bed she was suppose to unhook the screen door and then close and lock this back apartment door. One hot summer evening I came home and the screen door was still hooked from the inside. I quietly knocked on the screen door to wake her up. Being an apartment, I didn't want to make too much noise which would wake all the neighbors. When I couldn't wake her by knocking on the screen door I walked around to the front foyer entrance to the apartment and unlocked the front door, but the chain latch was hooked. The front foyer had a tremendous echo. So I called my wife's name softly through the chain latched door. No response! I called louder, still no response! Finally I yelled as loud as I could, nothing! I was reluctant to kick-in the front door, for it would make an awful lot of noise and we would be responsible for any damage to the doorframe. However, I was becoming worried, for I had a wife in this apartment and maybe something was wrong. I then went back around to the rear of the apartment, clawed my fingers under the edges of the screen door and ripped it off of it's hinges, making a terrible noise which brought on a number of my neighbors' apartment lights and many window blinds were spread to see what was happening. I'm sure most of them thought the young couple on the first floor was having a fight and she locked him out of the apartment. I went into the apartment bedroom and there was my lovely wife sound asleep. In a very loud frustrated voice I said, "Dianne, Dianne!" No response! I touched her and she immediately woke up, and said, "Hi honey", and then proceeded to pull cotton from her ears explaining she had had an ear ache and had put some drops in her ears before going to bed.

Forty-one years later at 2:30 AM, she wakes me up asking, "What is that loud noise?" It sounded to me as if one of our dogs in the garage was scratching on the washroom door. I assumed the dogs wanted to relieve themselves and wished to be let out into the backyard. I went down stairs, let the dogs out into the backyard and then realized I had locked myself out of the house. I repeatedly pounded three times on the washroom door to the house, the universal signal of distress. No response! Over and over I repeated the three sequenced pounding, no response! After five minutes of repeated pounding, I picked up the garage phone and dialed our phone number and hung up which causes our phone to ring. When it stopped ringing I assumed she had answered it but then immediately hung up for I couldn't get her to talk to me on the phone. Over and over I dialed our phone number only to hear it ring four times and then stop. After about ten minutes I hear a voice on the other side of the door asking, "Who's out there?" I yelled, "Your, blankety blank husband, open up!"

As I had went down to let the dogs out she immediately went back to bed, and later upon hearing the repeated pounding wondered what I was doing in the garage pounding at 3:00 AM in the morning.

After forty-one years of marriage I have learned something new, she still doesn't know that three shots being fired or three short pounding sounds is a universal signal of distress. I guess the Girl Scouts don't teach them that kind of stuff. When I was pounding I did think of sending three short pounds, three long pounds, and three short pounds, for SOS, but something in the back of my mind just knew that wouldn't get me anyplace. After the phone would ring four times the answering machine would answer and that explained why I couldn't get her to talk to me. She also wondered who was doing all that calling at that time in the morning and why wasn't I picking up the phone sooner. Oh well, I guess twice in forty-one years isn't too bad. Oh, the reason the dog was scratching in the first place was a small electrical storm, and that little bitch Madchen is afraid of thunder.

SIT DOWN, KIRSTEN

During a family backyard party two-year-old granddaughter Kirsten repeatedly stood up on a patio picnic table seat. Concerned that she might fall I told her a number of times to sit down. Each time I cautioned her, my voice became deeper and more stern. After my last very stern admonition, her mother Margaret rebuked her and said, "What did your grandfather just say to you?"

Mimicking me in the deepest voice her young vocal cords could muster, she growled, "SIT DOWN!"

It was obvious she heard and understood the admonitions, but in those moments compliance just wasn't her forte.

EVERYTHING WILL BE ALL RIGHT

It was September 23, 1993, three weeks before my Radical Prostectomy. The lady in my dream peered through the door of a little portal that had an arched ceiling. Half way through the door, she looked directly at me and said, "I have it from the highest authority, everything will be all right."

At this point I awoke and lying on my back in bed, I asked myself what did this dream mean? At first I was unhappy that the message wasn't more specific like, ...everything with regard to the forthcoming prostate operation will be all right. Then I realized that I had received a very all encompassing message for the future, "...everything will be all right"

Was the lady my (Jungian) animae? I didn't know who the lady in the dream was. Later I remembered that the name of our great city is, "The city of Our Lady Queen of the Angels of the Little Portal".

Needless to say when the time came for my Radical Prostatectomy, I was totally relaxed, for I knew in the deepest part of my psyche that everything would be all right.

Later in July 1994 when I had my rotary cuff operation on my left shoulder, I again knew everything would be all right.

In October 1997, I again knew beyond a shadow of a doubt that the quadruple heart by-pass would turn out all right. And again in July 1999 I knew beyond a shadow of a doubt that the removal of the tumor in my left lung would be all right-because the lady said so years before-"Everything will be all right!"

OLD MAN IN ST. MORITZ

Dianne and I were staying at the Hotel Steffani in St. Moritz, Switzerland for a couple of days prior to taking the Glacier Express to Zermatt.

The previous two weeks in July 1994 had been spent in Einseildeln near Zurich attending a Jungian seminar.

One afternoon we took a cable car to the top of the Corvatsch glacier.

On the way down an elderly gentleman, accompanied by a young lady, admired Dianne's camera and we struck up a conversation. He said he grew up in Alsace-Lorraine, a province in France that over the years has been alternately claimed by both France and Germany. He went on to say he was in three armies during the Second World War. First he was in the French army, then after the German occupation he was drafted into the German army because they felt anyone living in this province was always really a German. Finally he joined the American army near the end of World War II. We agreed this was very unusual. He asked us how long we planned to stay in the St. Moritz area and where were we staying? We parted at the bus stop and returned to our hotel.

That evening as we sat in the hotel dinning room, we observed the old man with the young lady walking past the hotel. After dinner we went for a brief walk. Upon returning we stopped at the hotel desk for our massive room key. This hotel's key, like many in Europe, were all attached to light bulb size brass weights that discouraged guests from carrying them off, and encouraged them to be left at the desk. When the desk clerk checked, he said our key was not in the box and questioned if we might have taken it out with us. We said no, and a search began. I mentioned we had definitely left the key at the desk when we came down for supper. The key was finally located at the extreme end of the counter, an out of place location.

Upon returning to our room, I wondered who may have obtained our key and what they may have taken from our room. We had our cameras, tickets and money with us, and nothing else appeared to be missing.

To this day I wonder if that old man or his young female friend entered our room and if we had left cameras or money in the room if they would have been missing.

Since then I have been careful not to give too much information to strangers.

GRANDPA'S HAIR

I asked four year old grandson Nicolas to rub my shoulders. He stood up on the sofa behind me and massaged my shoulders and neck for a couple minutes. I complimented him on what a good job he was doing, when he abruptly stopped. I could feel his fingers on the top of my head. His mother glanced over and asked him what he was doing? He replied, "Grandpa's head is growing out of his hair!"

WORD ASSOCIATION

Sixteen month old grandson Mark opened the doors to our pots and pans cabinet underneath our stove. Surveying this array of wonderful noise making implements, he held the doors open and clearly uttered the one descriptive word he'd learned to associate with these marvelous items, "getouttathere".

SATISFACTION

Sixteen-month-old grandson Mark clawed and pulled at the closet door until he opened it. He then pulled at one of two five gallon plastic buckets full of toys. I carried one of the buckets into the family room and closed the closet door, which has a simple magnetic latch. Surveying the bucket in the family room for a minute, he then returned to the closet and again managed to open the door and pulled at the second bucket of toys. After placing the second bucket in the family room, I again closed the closet door. Looking over the two buckets, this little man returned to the closet door and pulled on it until he had opened it a third time. Assuring himself that he had all the toys, he then returned to the family room and began the laborious task of dumping both buckets upside down onto the floor. Clearly, satisfaction is in the eyes of the beholder!

THE EXTRA HOTEL GUEST

Dianne and I spent a weekend at a seashore hotel about a hundred miles from our home. Our room was near the hotel tower. Around midnight, with my head on my pillow, I heard what sounded like a muffled bowling ball being dropped on the floor, thump, thump-a brief space of time, then bump, bump again. It was like a bowling ball being dropped and then bouncing slightly and hitting the floor again. When I lifted my head off of my pillow I could no longer hear the thumping sound. Being half asleep, I rolled over to think about this sound and promptly went back to sleep.

About an hour later I again awoke, and sensing Dianne was awake, I ask if anything was wrong? She asked if I could hear the footsteps next to the bed. I said, "No."

She said, "Lean over me, and put your head on my side of the bed".

When I leaned over her, I could hear the squeak-squeak of pacing footsteps along her side of the bed. It was as if someone were walking beside the bed. The pacing seemed to go to the foot of the bed and then back to the head of the bed-back and forth-back and forth. I couldn't hear the footsteps on my side of the bed, only when I leaned over her and placed my head on her side. Being sleepy and reluctant to become fully awake, and seeing no visible signs, I laid back down thinking the pacing might be coming from the hallway and again dropped off to sleep.

I learned the next morning, that Dianne couldn't go back to sleep and remained awake for an hour or more. She said she even got up and closed a closet door, thinking maybe the pacing sound was coming from the next room. In the morning I asked some of the hotel personnel if they could explain the phenomena. They seemed reluctant to discuss the subject of ghosts. The next two nights I was prepared to wake up promptly and scientifically examine this occurrence, but nothing more happen. About a year later I read an article in the paper about the tower ghost of the famous Hotel Del Coronado in San Diego, California.

(A couple years later I converted the above Hotel Del Coronado vignette into a short story as follows.)

THE EXTRA HOTEL GUEST
A Fictional Short Story by Roger J. Miller

"Do you hear it now?"

"Yes," I whispered as I laid back down for a moment to collect my thoughts. My eyes were still quite heavy with sleep as I closed them for a moment to think about this strange occurrence happening right next to the bed. What was going on here? Was this a ghost?

We had driven a hundred miles to this beach front hotel early this afternoon. When we made our reservations we requested an ocean view room. Upon arrival I made the mistake of failing to reaffirm this request to the desk clerk, so when the porter showed us into our room my wife immediately complained as she looked out the window.

"This isn't an ocean view room, it is at the back overlooking the hotel dumpsters!"

The young porter immediately picked-up on her complaint and volunteered to call the desk to obtain a more satisfactory room.

I have noted over my numerous senior accumulated years that porters are always very solicitous and accommodating when it comes to helping to straighten out a guest's complaint, for they are always hoping for a larger gratuity; whereas a complaint to the desk clerk usually evokes a, "We'll put your request in the computer and let you know if and when we have another opening, for all of our rooms are booked for tonight." Moving a guest always seems to be done reluctantly. Tipping the desk clerk isn't a well established American custom, but I've often wondered if passing five or ten dollars to the desk clerk might hasten the materialization of the requested room change.

The young porter did call the desk and within minutes we had a new room on the other side of the hotel providing a view of the beach and ocean to the west of the hotel. He got an extra good tip.

Our new room was at the end of the hall on the top floor to the west of the tower. The room had a narrow "L" shape, with a double bed squeezed between the hall door and an outside wall, with the head of the bed resting against the wall common to the hallway. At the foot of the bed there was ample room for a small table, chairs and a TV. The bathroom occupied the lower leg of the "L". While the room had a peculiar narrow shape, we found it satisfactory and it did give us our desired ocean view, as well as a view of a westerly sunset. I later looked back on this easily accomplished room change and wondered if this room was only assigned as a last resort, when nothing else was available and guests were vehemently complaining.

All the restaurants were crowded that evening resulting in a late supper and a late return to our room. We watched a movie and went to bed about eleven thirty. My wife has had a lot of foot and back problems and always wants to sleep on the side of the bed offering the most direct access to the bathroom to avoid stumbling around in the dark in an unfamiliar room.

Of the two of us, I tend to be more excitable, but I also tend to be more questioning and analytical. She on the other hand can be very calm in stressful situations, due to a large extent to her extensive hospital work and psychological training. Shrinks, always seem to handle stress a little bit better than us average mortals. I tend to fall asleep very easily, and usually sleep through the night with only occasional short wakeful periods. She on the other hand, has trouble getting to sleep due to her physical discomforts and often has long wakeful periods during the night.

I dropped off to sleep first and slowly woke up after about an hour to a thumping sound. I laid there with one ear to the pillow listening to the thumping which seemed to originate from below the pillow. Being a little hard of hearing, I often have to raise up to use both ears to locate the direction of a sound, especially when I have been laying down in bed. I raised up on an elbow, but I heard nothing! Finding the sound to be gone, I laid back down on the pillow. There it was again! "Thump, thump", like a bowling ball bouncing on a hard carpeted floor, with the initial thump being somewhat louder than the secondary thump. With my head lying on the pillow I could hear the sound, but when I raised up off the pillow I could not hear anything. Very, very strange I thought. The pillow should be dampening the sound not amplifying it. This situation was completely contradictory to what I would normally expect to happen. I would think the pillow would dampen the sound and when I raised up I should be able to hear more clearly any sound in the room or nearby. But the sound in this situation was just the opposite. Curious, but still sleepy, I tried to find a position where the thumping didn't bother me that much and then tried to go back to sleep, thinking it was probably just an unusual phenomenon of the walls and structure of this late 19th Century hotel. It didn't fit my established thinking pattern, but as I grow older and as the world rapidly changes, I'm trying to remember not to try to force fit everything that's different into my known frame of reference.

About an hour after the thumping incident I awoke again as I felt my wife stir next to me. It was a somewhat nervous movement that prompted me to ask if she was awake, since she had been having recent back trouble.

She responded, "Do you hear the footsteps?"

"No! What footsteps?"

"I can hear footsteps right next to my side of the bed!" she whispered.

"I can't hear a thing!"

"Lean over me and listen!" she whispered again.

As I leaned over her placing my head on her side of the bed, I could hear firm padded footsteps pacing to and fro along the side of the bed. The sound was a combination of a foot on the rug coupled with a faint squeak of the wood floor beneath. The pacing would slowly move to the foot of the bed, then return to the head of the bed and then slowly return to the foot of the bed... back and forth,... back and forth,...but I could not see anything!

My wife whispered, "Maybe it's someone out in the hall walking back and forth".

I didn't think so, for those footsteps were clearly right next to the bed. If a person had been walking in those footsteps he or she or it would have bumped or brushed my head as they or it had walked by, for I had been leaning that far out over the side of the bed. At no time did I have any sense or feeling of danger or fear. My eye lids were still very heavy, so I kept them closed while I thought about what to do next-and woke up the next morning with the fresh ocean sunlight shining through the window and the sound of seagulls nearby.

Oh boy! I had fallen back to sleep, what happened after I went back to sleep?

I waited until my wife woke up and I immediately asked, "I guess I fell asleep after I leaned over and heard the footsteps, what happen after that?"

She said she laid there somewhat anxious but not really frightened and not quite sure what to do next. After a while she said she got up and closed the closet door thinking maybe the sound was coming from the next room. She said the footsteps continued for over half an hour and eventually stopped as quietly as they had started. I asked her if she'd heard anything else, like the guests screaming down the hall, indicating the ghostly visitor had moved on to other rooms.

I reminded her of the time we were all at Yellow Stone National Park and the grizzly bear visited the adjacent campsite and beat open a cooler that had been left out on a table to get at freshly caught fish. After the bear's visit, I had laid awake for hours, until I faintly heard people screaming, "Bear..bear.." far off in the distance and I knew our Bruin visitor had moved on to some one else's exposed cooler.

"No, nothing like that!" she curtly replied.

I began to think of various tests I should have conducted, like standing next to the bed and allowing the footsteps and or the entity to pass through a foot or hand to see if I could sense anything, like a chill or heat or some other sensation. I also should have opened the hall door to convince myself that no one was walking or causing the thumping sound or the footstep out in the hall. I also thought of asking the desk clerk if any ghostly phenomenon had been reported or occurred before this.

I glibly told my wife, "If any ghost wants me to believe in it, it better glow a respectable ghoulish green to prove it's an authentic ghost, for after all, all of Disney's ghosts glow a respectable green."

She gave me a cold stare! Sometimes she doesn't fully appreciate my attempts at humor.

On the way down to breakfast, I asked the elevator operator if there had been any ghostly apparitions reported in the hotel. He looked at us strangely, and at that moment I immediately decided not to press the questioning any further with the desk clerk. He probably wouldn't have admitted anything anyway. Later that day we did find out that the room next to us had been unoccupied the previous night.

Our first day was the usual touristy togetherness of the wife looking in all the shops, bar none, as the husband boringly follows, praying quietly to himself that she won't find too many precious dust collecting somethings that we'll have to desperately try to get home unbroken. I never cease to be amazed at the variety of the little somethings that one gender can glance over from the shop's doorway and be eternally satisfied that he has not missed anything important, while the other gender cannot reach this same level of complete confidence until the perimeter of each and every table and wall of the shop has been thoroughly inspected. Needless to say, the examination of the hotel shops required an extensive amount of time and took most of our first day, leaving the visit to the city's Old Town and its shops to the second day.

We did have a delightful conversation with a senior lady in one of the shops that knew a lot about the hotel's history. I inquired if the hotel had any interesting legends, and she proudly replied, "Oh yes, we have a ghost in one of the west tower rooms; but the room is never rented out unless we are really overbooked, because some people have occasionally reported hearing a ghost pacing the floor. It seems a young newly married couple rented the room around the turn of the century for their honeymoon night. The husband went down to get some champagne, but was forced to walk a distance to get the spirits and along the way he was mugged and murdered. The young wife, whose name was Maria, frighten and confused, paced the floor all night waiting for a husband that never returned. It is said she returned on the same day a month later and rented the same room. The coroner said she died that night of natural causes, but many say it was from a broken heart. It's been reported numerous times over the years that footsteps and noises are heard in the wee hours of the morning in and around that room."

Upon getting ready for bed the second night I mentally thought through all the various acceptable investigative type examinations that I was going to conduct if and when any phenomenon occurred the next two nights. Such as, I will definitely get up out of a nice warm bed and look out in the hall. I will get down on the floor and examine the footsteps as they walk by, assuming of course this phenomenon has a defined route that it visits on a routine basis, rather than once in a millennium. I will see if turning on the lights stops or bothers the entity. I will see if I can feel any sensation as the ghost walks past or through me. I will not be lazy and fall back to sleep without properly examining this interesting and unusual experience to the fullest extent possible. All of this I promised myself.

The second night absolutely nothing happen, nary a squeak. Or if anything did happen, neither my wife nor I woke up to hear or see it. But on our last night as I prepared for bed I spilled some foot powder on the bathroom floor. I decided to go to bed and to wipe it up in the morning. In the early morning hours my wife got up to go to the bathroom and excitedly called to me, "Honey, come here quick, come here!"

As I peered into the bathroom, there on the floor were what I would describe as slipper prints in the foot powder, as if someone had walked into the bathroom. My wife quickly pointed out the slipper size appeared to be about three sizes smaller than hers. She quietly said, "The ghost is here in the room, still waiting for her lover. I'm going to try and help her."

"You're going to do what?" I responded.

With that she began to firmly speak to the ghost saying, "Maria, go towards the light! Maria, go towards the light, your husband is waiting for you! Go towards the light at the end of the tunnel." She repeated these phrases for about five minutes.

We heard nor saw anything else and we went back to bed. About four AM my wife woke me and asked, "Do you smell anything?"

I said, "Yes, I smell a whole lot of Roses."

My wife satisfied said, "I think Maria, has been reunited with her husband. I don't think she'll be pacing the floor in this room anymore."

As time passed my wife and I generally forgot the incident, except when sharing the story with friends. The whole weekend came back in vivid detail a few years later when the LA Times ran a story one Sunday morning about the various ghosts occupying our southland and mentioned that their once had been a tower ghost in the Hotel Del Coronado in San Diego, California, but it hadn't been heard for some time.

LEBENS LAUF

In a "Singles" meeting in '53,
I met a young lady from far away,
the very first night I felt she was neat,
we went to the Long Beach *pike* for some play.

That summer was beach parties and much fun,
group outings to mountains and sailing boats,
we were all single, young and unattached,
who played together, just feeling our oats.

Although we were all having very much fun, all through
that summer there was a slight "hitch",
this beautiful young lady was engaged,
to one who had made an earlier "pitch".

Then after school one evening in the Fall,
I noticed her engagement ring was gone,
a quick query brought a hopeful reply,
her freedom woke for me a bright new dawn.

I asked her to a Mass the next Sunday,

and in the evening we went to a show,
I kissed her that night, kind of missed a mile,
that's OK, I still went home with a glow.

We dated and talked a lot in those days,
and as we talked she learned all about me,
while I heard about family and friends,
and all the things that she wanted to be.

We discussed marriage and settling down,
yet I still had to finish years of school,
and she said that long drawn out engagements,
definitely did not fit in her rule.

Relatives discouraged a union then,
for I had no degree, job, or money.
She said if it was to be a long wait,
 it was back to Portland for my honey.

For the next few months we dated a lot,
 I gave her a ring and asked for her hand,
we set the date for the ninetieth of June,
that was the day set for the wedding band.

We came together the nineteenth of June,
a most beautiful and all in white bride,
a nervous yet anticipating groom,
both expectant filled with love, joy and pride.

The wedding was all over very quick,
then as we stood, my bride deserted me,
to place a bouquet on Mary's altar,
her absence seemed like an eternity.

We then retired to Saint Barnabas hall,
for a reception with guests and my wife,
when boys carried my bride right out the door,
it appeared my marriage would start with strife.

In a while they returned the kidnapped wife,
wedding pictures were taken in the church,
then we changed and prepared to travel,
but first we had to leave friends in the lurch.

My brother and friends chased us all over town,
we eluded them by running through stores,
gained our car from a underground garage,
 then drove toward Santa Barbara's shores.

Santa Barbara was reached early that day,
Santa Maria was our final stop,
we asked for a room far back from the road,
I thought the bed was a great place to drop.

But my new wife had other ideas,
she insisted upon then being fed,
this she said was a firm requirement,
before I would get her into a bed.

On our second night we stopped in Carmel,
later on we camped at Yosemite,
my new bride did not complain that much,
 when the camping did not fit her to a tee.

At Yosemite we went for a hike,
my brand new wife did not wear any socks,
 blisters were the product of that long walk,
which left a score of hiking mental blocks.

We started out with two hundred dollars,
but ten dollars was lost along the way,
this financial disaster and the hike,
thus caused a shortened Yosemite stay.

We came back to our Wardlow apartment,
 I worked at a small market for low pay,
we found out soon that Di was expecting,
a full time job was needed right away.

We moved from our Wardlow apartment quick,
 for my mom kept dropping by unannounced,
closer to Cal State U. was our desire,
we stayed there til Number Two was pronounced.

We sure needed help from the GI Bill,
so that La Mirada could be our home,
three bedrooms and a den gave us the space,
needed for the young family to roam.

THE POETIC REBUTTAL

There once was a class of writers,
who at times were bored by their peers.
When Roger wrote about batteries,
it drove teacher Edwards to tears.

When Betty Edwards and her class,
 heard all about battery grounds,
the class interest really waned,
and teacher boredom knew no bounds.

Now this type of peer reception,
might discourage a lesser man,
but one must always remember,
this problem's not new to your van.
When battery problems are here,
 it can cause a person much strife,
and if one offers solutions,
he can be told to *get-a-life*.

Often when these things are discussed,
some of our peer's eyes become *glazed*.
This does not portend non-interest,
but shows them becoming amazed.

If you still can't *buy* this logic,
and this answer's not your forte,
then wait for your dead battery,
for it will come along any day.

But if you choose to be careful,
and if you wish to be prepared,
then carefully store in your trunk,
battery cables to be paired.

And when that foul day finally comes,
and when that starter tick, tick, ticks,
then withdraw from your trunk cables,
and transfer a charge that'll do tricks.

And if the engine hesitates,
then once again enhance that ground,
with more and more ground connections,
which will make that engine go round.

This solution surely won't fail,
not when it's properly applied,
just enhance that electron path,
and don't worry about what's died.

MY HONEY'S LUMBAR LAMINECTOMY

At five-thirty we made St. Jude a stop,
for Di's Lumbar Laminectomy Op.
Sister Judith, Di and I said a prayer,
that angels would surround the Op Room air.

We prayed that angels would guide surgeons' hands,
correcting the Lumbar with bone and bands.
I sat in the lobby writing this theme,
imagining angels on this Op team.

Father Larry came by to offer prayers,
reminding me of God's many awares.
The surgery is long and I'm anxious,
trying to keep good thoughts in my conscious.

Father Bill and Judith paid a visit,
praying for Di, while I am in respite.
I keep imagining healing angels,
watching this procedure from all angles.

By 10 A.M. the time sure has been long,
I hope to soon see surgeons come along.
I know the Op can be hours of work,
I must not be restless or go berserk!

Marque called saying that she's on the way,
to sit with me and to help pass this day.

It's eleven-thirty, four hours have passed,
seeing the Doctors now would be a blast!

Debbie called, she didn't have the five hour view,
I'm to call her if I have anything new.
Francis just came to say they're finishing,
it's twelve-thirty, we're in the last inning.

Though I have been really very uptight,
Doctor Kropf just said everything's all right.

CONCERNED BABIES

Recently my youngest daughter Margaret's mother-in-law broke her ankle. Shortly thereafter Dianne had a lumbar laminectomy and fusion. My five year old grandson observed that both of his grandmothers had the same four-legged aluminum walkers. He thought that was very interesting. A week later his three year old sister inquired very sympathetically, "Grandpa, how is grandma's ankle?" I then explained that your daddy's mother broke her ankle, while your mommy's mother has a back that hurts. Both grandchildren looked at me very seriously, slowly digesting the fact that both of their grandmothers didn't have the same kind of injury, considering the fact that they both had the same kind of aluminum walkers.

A GERMAN VERSION OF SNOW WHITE

Spiegelen Spiegelen an der Wand,
Wer ist die schoneste im ganzen Land,

Frau Konigen, sie ist die schoneste hier,
aber ober dem Bergen,
bei die sieben Zwergen,

ist Schnee Witchen,

und Sie ist nach tausend mal schoner aus ihr.

DON'T ARGUE WITH RUFUS

My brother and family live in the San Bernardino mountains in southern California. My sister-in-law worked in a large camp lodge as a cook. A few years back they were allowed the use the lodge for a wedding reception for their daughter. Part of the deal with the cooks was cleaning up the dishes and kitchen after it was all over, which was an awesome job. I helped out washing dishes for a couple hours. We were almost finished and my brother asked me to take the garbage fifty yards down the trail to the trash cans. He handed me a flashlight and told me to make sure and put the trash can lit on real tight. Then he said casually, "Oh by the way if Rufus wants the garbage give it to him!"

I looked at him and said, "Who's Rufus?"

He laughingly replied, "A real big black bear."

Needless to say I moved quickly and quietly watching every shadow all the way down and back. I talked to my brother recently and he said Rufus can still be heard usually a couple times a week *banging* the lids off trash cans in the early hours of the morning..

OH OH!

I felt a little flushed and eyed the monitor as the technician said, "Oh, Oh!"

When one is having his first Angiogram and is extremely apprehensive of the whole procedure-and even though your wife says there's nothing to it-my anxiety spiked through the roof with that, "Oh Oh!"

A few minutes later, Dr. Borsari gave me the bad news, four blocked arteries, a couple almost 99% closed. He said, "No cruise!"

Dianne and I were planning on leaving the next week on a twelve day New England fall foliage cruise from Boston to the Maritime Provinces of Canada.

As weights and pressure were applied to my groin area to ensure that the artery they used during the procedure would close properly, I lay in a critical care room considering the doctor's suggestion that I undergo an immediate quadruple heart by-pass the next morning. Shortly thereafter Dr. Tovar, a surgeon, came in and said he would be available to do the surgery the next morning. As the day progressed I was having some angina like pain.

A neck sonogram was made on my carotid arteries and showed a 90% blockage on the left side. Dr. Tovar came back in and said they thought it would be a good idea to do the surgery that afternoon.

The technician's "Oh, Oh!" turned into a very busy day. Around midnight, seven hours later, I'm told they rolled me back into the critical care area with a cleaned out left carotid artery and four veins routing around four blockages in heart arteries.

One has to be concerned with those "Oh, Oh's!"

THE TROOPERS

At a family gathering in Grand Island, Nebraska, Dale, my son Dennis's father-in-law looked up as the uniformed trooper said, "If you ever do that again I'm going to give you a ticket!"

Dale roared with laughter.

Later I asked, "What was that all about?"

Dale, a veteran driver of eighteen wheelers, replied that he saw two state troopers waiting at a traffic light about a week ago. As he made a left turn in front of them he flipped them the finger.

The trooper who was in the passenger seat asked, "Did you see that?"

The cruiser driver dejectedly answered, "Yes."

"Well, are you going after him?"

Back came a reluctant, "No!"

"Why not?"

"Cause he's my Grandpa."

OK MOMMIE PUT HIM BACK

As my two and a half year old grandson was introduced to his less than an hour old brother, his mother said, "See Kevin, baby Timothy has come out of mamma's tummy. Would you like to hold him?"

Kevin sat in a chair and his mother cradled the new born in his arms. After a minute or so of holding his new brother, Kevin said, "OK, mommy, put him back (in your tummy)!"

NO PEOPLE

Dianne, I, Mary and Debbie and families were at Pinecrest Lake in August 1999. It was the week before Fall school was to commence. The teenage girls were all laying out on the beach frying their young skin into something akin to brown leather, while some of us adults were hiding from the sun in the shade of hundred foot pine trees.

Tamara said, "Mom, next year we have to come two weeks earlier when there are some people here!"

I looked up and down the beach - families basking on the sand - kids playing in the water - sail boats racing farther out - fishing boats spotted all over the lake, anything but a place void of people. I said, "What do you mean, no people, there's people all over this crowded beach!"

Mary, with a mother's wisdom, looked over toward me and said, "Boys, Dad, she means there's no boys here this week. They've all left to get ready for school."

CHECKERS

Nine year old granddaughter Jacqueline and I were playing Checkers. She had already beaten me a couple games and I was being very careful not to lose this game. As I reached for a piece, Jacqueline said, "I wouldn't make that move if I were you, Grandpa."

I considered what she had just said and answered, "What's wrong with it? It's a good move!"

She politely answered, "I wouldn't make it if I were you."

I made the move anyway, and in two more moves she jumped three of my pieces and got a King. She looked at me, smiled again politely and said, "Told you it wasn't a good move!" That afternoon I never did win a game.

A THREE AND A HALF YEAR
OLD'S PRONUNCIATION

A mother down the street called daughter Therese and said, "Your son is telling my children that he wants to be a drunk driver when he grows up."

When little Jacob came home Therese asked him to tell her

what he wanted to be when he grew up and he said, "A dunt driver, Mommie!"

She carefully instructed him at what she perceived to be a three and a half year old level on why he shouldn't aspire to be a drunk driver. When she was finished, she said, "Now what do you want to be when you grow up?"

He said, "A dunt driver, Mommie!"

Trying a different tack, she said, "What do you think drunk drivers do?"

He said, They jump over other cars, they crash into other cars, they race other cars."

She said, "You mean a stunt driver."

Yes Mommie, a dtunt driver."

Some time later little Jacob asked to be read to before he went to sleep. Therese asked him what story he would like to hear. He said, "No book, Mommie."

She asked again, "What do you want me to read to you?"

He said, "No book."

"If you don't want me to read a book, what do you want me to read?"

"A no book, Mommie."

She said, "Jacob, I don't know what you want."

The exasperated little three and a half year old put both hands on his hips, looked his mother straight in the eye and said, "A S-s-s-s-s NO book, Mommie!"

"You mean a snow book story?"

"Yes, Mommie."

Therese remarked later, "After the stunt driver episode, I should have picked up on the snow book quicker!"

VALENTINE'S DAY 2000

'Tis the fourteenth of February,
in the second month of a Leap Year,
creating a heart felt sentiment,
writing rhymes for my honey to hear.

Outside it's raining and inclement,
inside Dianne's hard at her quilting,
while I am attempting this sonnet,
as my gift and Valentine offering.

'Tis our forty-sixth Valentine day,
which gives a good excuse to make hay,
so, whatever we decide to play,
it'll be easy to make it pay.

And I'm sure by the end of this day,
we will have proved together we stay.

A GRANDSON'S QUESTIONS

My wife and I were having lunch with Therese and Marque and some of their children. Therese was four months pregnant expecting her fourth child and hoping for a girl. She asked her four year old son Jacob what would he like-a boy or a girl. Jacob indicated he wished for a boy. His mother asked him what he would do if it was a girl?

He answered, "Dress her like a boy!"

After lunch was finished, Jacob looked up at his mother and said,

"Mommy, does all the food you eat just pile up on top of the baby's head?"

OBSERVING LITTLE BOYS AND LITTLE GIRLS

We installed an old fashioned toilet with a water tank hung high on the wall above the toilet bowl. To flush a person must pull a chain hanging from the water tank. Dianne and I thought this would be a quaint addition to our downstairs bathroom. Wrong! First of all not enough water is released with one jerk of the chain fast enough to accomplish a clean and total flush due to the size of the pipe running from the tank - thus requiring a second flush. Or as we discovered in time – holding down the chain thus allowing all the water to empty from the tank does a better job of flushing. Some people catch on fast, others make repeated flushes.

The grandchildren have been interesting to watch when they use this old fashioned arrangement. Generally the grandsons appear to have less trouble. When the little boys are ready to flush they look around and see no handle to flush the toilet. They stand there a moment, looking this different toilet over, then put down the lid, climb up and pull down on the chain. Not one of the grandsons has asked what to do. Whereas the granddaughters come out of the bathroom confused as to how to flush this old toilet.

Why do the little boys have less difficulty? Apparently they observe and then figure out what to do. The granddaughters observe but don't seem to take the next step in the solution. Maybe it has something to do with mechanical aptitude.

1953-LBCC Prom

2005-Dianne Miller and Snuggles

CHAPTER 11
My Seventies
(The 2000's)

My Genealogy
My Father's Side

I don't know much about my father's side of the family. He died when I was ten and I failed to talk to my Dad's two younger sisters (Aunts Meta and Esther) while they were still alive about the Miller family history. My mother related a story about the original name being Mueller, and that it had been changed during the early part of the twentieth century to prevent mail getting mixed up. If my mother related the story it must have come from my Dad, for I doubt anyone else would have made the story up. Sometimes verbal history is some of the best sources even though it cannot be backed up by printed references.

My paternal grandfather was Joseph W. Miller (Mueller), born in Coastville, Clayton County, Iowa, in November 1871, married in Hartford, South Dakota, April 1897, and died in Long Beach, California, January 17, 1949. He belonged to the Lutheran church. He spent most of his adult life as a farmer in Hartford, South Dakota, retiring in Long Beach in the 1920's. As a ten year old all I remember my grandfather doing is sitting in a high backed chair looking out the window. He never seemed to go anyplace. This was a false impression, for my mother told me he often spent some days at the Long Beach University by the Sea (better known as the Spit-and-Argue Club) located at the north end of Rainbow Pier, listening to the never ending debates on every subject imaginable. My grandfather suffered from diabetes that did limit his getting out. Visiting my grandparents was boring! They owned an apartment building with two one-bedroom apartments upstairs and two downstairs. They lived in one of the apartments and rented out the other three. There was an enclosed front stairs and a steep exposed rear stairs that we were always cautioned to be careful going down. There was an inside window in the hallway leading to the one back bedroom. The window opened on a laundry chute that dropped soiled clothes right into the first floor laundry room. Of course we were continually cautioned not to get up on the windowsill for fear we would fall down the chute. We were cautioned about the steep back stairs, and about running through the apartment making noise that might disturb the residents on the ground floor. We were cautioned about running up and down the enclosed front stairs that might disturb the first floor people. The living room had a closet that when opened exposed a double hide-a-way bed and a built in chest of drawers which reminded my brother David and me of a secret room. We were cautioned not to get into any of the chest of drawers. Needless to say visits to grandpa and grandma's apartment was boring and I was always a reluctant visitor.

My paternal great grandfather was Joseph Mueller, and great grandmother was Fredericka (Freida), maiden name not remembered.

I remember my mother mentioning an Uncle Benjamin, a brother of my great grandfather or my great great grandfather, who was born in Germany and came to the USA after the initial Muellers arrived in this country. This individual may have been the person from which my father got his middle name.

My paternal grandmother was Mary B. Englehardt, born in Clayton

County, Iowa in 1877, and died in Long Beach, California, February 8, 1956. Her parents were Wilhelm Julius and Louisa Englehardt.

My grandparents, Joseph W. and Mary B. Miller had three children, Meta, Esther, and my dad Roy Benjamin Miller, born February 9, 1899 in Hartford, South Dakota. He and my mother were married June 15, 1928 in a rectory in Santa Ana, California, because he was not Catholic and a Lutheran

My dad and mother honeymooned in Yosemite, staying in the Camp Curry tent accommodations right near the famous nightly fire fall from Glacier Point. They drove to Yosemite in my dad's Star Roadster via the old Los Angeles to Bakersfield ridge route road that took a whole day to navigate.

Roy B. Miller worked for Arden Farms. Shortly after their marriage they moved to Santa Catalina Island where he was the sole milkman for the small village of Avalon. I was born in St. Mary's hospital in Avalon, July 23, 1930. My dad, being a farm boy from South Dakota, was always very frightened of earthquakes. Just after the 1933 Long Beach quake, he was certain the island might get hit by a tidal wave and moved his family to the mainland. In Long Beach he drove a large refrigeration truck delivering ice cream and milk to grocery and drug stores in the small towns surrounding Long Beach. My ten-year-old memories of my dad have long ago faded into just few brief facts.

My two growing up homes were 3625 Walnut Avenue and 3569 Gaviota Avenue. My mother wanted to own her own home. Unbeknownst to my father, she used her $250.00 inheritance from her family home to purchase the lot on Gaviota. Once the lot was purchased, she convinced my dad to get a Federal Housing Authority (FHA) loan to build the house.

My dad died from a blood clot in the brain on October 21, 1940, my mother's birthday. My mother related that on the day of his death, a Monday, she was in the garage doing washing when her sister Therese and Tracy Bragg, a former co-worker of my dad, came walking down our driveway toward her. She jokingly inquired what the two of them were doing out together at that time of day. They gave her the news that my dad had fallen over on his route and died on the spot.

As I rode my bike home from school that afternoon my mom was standing in the front yard waiting for my brother David and I. She told us our father had died that afternoon. Neighborhood ladies were in the house talking. I just sat down in the house shocked. David who was eight finally went out and played with some of our friends in the front yard. I didn't want to play. I just sat in the house. I'm not real sure I remember anymore what my thoughts were.

Little Leroy was only two and didn't remember much of what happen. David and I wanted to sleep with my mom for weeks afterward. I remember the funeral was crowded and the line of cars was very long going to the mausoleum. David touched my dad in the coffin, I was afraid and would not touch him. Leroy didn't go to the funeral, for my mom felt it was best he didn't see his father in death. She told him Daddy went away on a train. For months afterward when Leroy heard a train whistle, he would ask, "Daddy come mommy? Daddy come?"

My Mother's Side

My mother's side of the family is a bit easier to document; Ursula Pauline Burggraff was born October 21, 1901 in North Prairie, Minnesota. She died in a La Habra, California convalescent hospital on May 31, 1991 of heart and kidney failure.

My maternal grandfather, my mother's father, was Charles Burggraff, born March 3, 1869, in Two Rivers Township, Morrison County, Minnesota and died July 26, 1924 in Little Falls, Minnesota of blood poisoning from an infected thumb, cut while trimming a horse's hoof, while working on the Blanchard Rapids dam. His parents were Johann and Josephine Burggraff.

Johann Burggraff was born near Luxemburg, Germany on February 22, 1832; and Josephine (Schackman) was born February 2, 1829 in Belgium. Johann and Josephine were married in 1853 in Germany, and then immigrated via Canada, then Michigan, to St. Cloud, Minnesota. Johann and Josephine were blessed with nine children, Nicholas born in 1854 in Canada, Mary born in 1857 in Canada, Henry born 1859 in Canada, Bertha born in 1861, Christina born in 1863 in Michigan, John Jr. born in 1865 in Minnesota, Elizabeth born in 1866 in Minnesota, my grandfather Charles born in 1869 in Two Rivers Township, in Morrison County, Minnesota, and Martin born in 1870 in Minnesota. In 1867 they built a log cabin and barn on an 80-acre homestead south of North Prairie in Brockway Township. After five years they had to leave the farm because their homestead papers were not correct. Subsequently, Johann bought 100 acres in Two Rivers Township South of North Prairie. There on the Spunk River, Johann built a sawmill that he operated for approximately twelve years until 1884, at which time a flood destroyed it. He rebuilt on the same spot and sometime later converted the site into a flourmill that was the first mill in Morrison County. Farmers brought wheat by horse and oxen from many miles away to have it ground into flour. Johann later sold the mill and bought 200 acres in Two Rivers where he farmed until he was 58 years old, at which time he divided the farm between his sons John Jr. and Charles (my grandfather). In 1890, he moved to North Prairie where he built the sacristy for the first log church in North Prairie and where he resided until his death in May 1902. Josephine died in February 1903. They both are buried side by side in the Catholic cemetery at North Prairie.

My Grandfather Charles Burggraff, was baptized at North Prairie by an itinerant missionary who often preached in the area. He received his schooling at North Prairie. His teachers were Mr. Hymont, Mr. Donat Trettel and Mr. Roble. Charles quit school at 16 years and started working in George Geisel's store in North Prairie for about five years. After that he helped his father with the farm work. When his father bequeathed him eighty acres, he built a frame house, a log barn and other farm out buildings. He later purchased an additional forty acres of school land. He used horses on his farm right from the very start. Charles Burggraff improved his farm and later sold it to Frank Sobiech for $1,800. After he sold the farm he became a store proprietor in North Prairie until his father died in 1902, at which time he moved onto his late father's farm. In 1911, he bought an improved farm one mile north of North Prairie for $7,000. This farm was inherited by his son Justus and is the farm I remember most from my childhood.

My maternal grandmother was Suzanna Thomalla, born April 12, 1869 in Krogulno Village, in Upper Silesia, Prussia, which today is in a part of Poland. She and her family immigrated to the US in 1871. The voyage took twenty-one days and upon arrival they kept going west until they reached North Prairie, Morrison County, Minnesota. Her parents were Charles and Johanna Thomalla. Johanna's maiden name was Misterek.

Charles Thomalla was born February 18, 1824, in Krogulno, Upper Silesia, Prussia (which is now Poland) and died January 22, 1901, and buried in the North Prairie Catholic cemetery. Johanna (Anna) Misterek was born May 12, 1823 in Krogulno and died April 15, 1904 and is also buried in the North Prairie church cemetery. They had five children, Anna (Hannah) born in 1846 in Krogulno, Mary born in 1860 in Krogulno, Suzanna (my grandmother) born in 1869 in Krogulno, Frances born in 1875 in North Prairie and Joseph born in 1877 in North Prairie. Shortly after their arrival in 1871, Charles Thomalla purchased 40 acres in the Two Rivers Township. In 1881, he bought another 40 acres of railroad land and farmed these 80 acres until his death. Charles initially harvested his grain by scythe and cradle, and later with a binder. Threshing was done by horsepower initially and later with a wood burning steam powered threshing rig. Besides his farm work, he used to buy oxen and break (train) them for work.

Suzanna Thomalla attended the North Prairie School until she was fourteen years old and then worked at home until she was seventeen, at which time she worked on a farm near St. Cloud and later for a doctor in Royalton doing housework until she married Charles Burggraff on July 1, 1890. The Reverend Edward Nagle witnessed Charles and Suzanna in their marriage vows.